The Fall I Fell

First published in Great Britain in 2026 by
Electric Monkey, part of Farshore

An imprint of HarperCollins*Publishers*
1 London Bridge Street, London SE1 9GF

farshore.co.uk

HarperCollins*Publishers*
Macken House, 39/40 Mayor Street Upper,
Dublin 1, D01 C9W8

ISBN 978 0 00 883069 4
Printed and bound in the UK using 100% renewable electricity
at CPI Group (UK) Ltd
1

The Fall I Fell

MEGAN CLAWSON

For anyone missing home –
wherever or whoever that may be.

PROLOGUE

Two years ago

The floor of the treehouse never made a good bed. The cold planks, smoothed by years of growing feet, groaned as I stretched against their grain. I blinked into sunlight that blinded me through the gaps in the roof. Yet, somehow, that was the best sleep I had had in weeks. Perhaps it was the exhaustion of yesterday, or maybe all of the nights I'd laid awake crying had finally caught up to me. Still, I stayed there, on those planks, just a little while longer, ignoring the aching of my joints.

For just a moment, I didn't remember. Wrapped up in the light, the smell of the last dregs of summer air coming in through the window, I clung to those fleeting moments of rest that had been so rare of late. Then, like a change in the wind, it all came flooding back. Granny. Her life's most precious photos and the letters in that box that lay scattered around me. Jacob's arms holding me in the dark, and his lips, and the feeling of finally—

I sat up and called his name, though I already knew from the draught about me that I was alone. The night before played in my mind, in fragments at first, of dances, of tears, of quiet embraces, of lips too desperate to wait any longer. Then I remembered it so clearly. I could feel the touch of him on my skin as the exhaustion took us both and I fell asleep in his arms, and he stayed. He had stayed. I looked for any sign of him out of the window. The September morning clung to the warmth of the summer, but the leaves and their dying orange tips told the real story. The farm was yet to stir. Silence fell across the landscape, and Jacob was still nowhere to be seen.

Many times in my life I had questioned whether he was just a dream, but this time I knew that all of it was real, painfully real. He had been here. He had held me, kissed me, *loved* me. Surely, that meant something. He was no phantom, and it was no dream, so why was it that I was alone?

All the pieces of Granny's memories that were scattered around the floor quivered against one another in the breeze, hissing in whispered conversation. I gathered them as carefully as I could, saving the stray sheets from being carried away in the wind. No matter how hard I tried to coax the lid back onto the shoe box, it wouldn't sit flat. The sight of it, fit to burst with photos a plenty, was rather fitting. Granny's life was far too full to fit into any box.

Then, from the corner of my eye, I spotted it.

A single sheet of paper, crumpled into a ball, tucked in the shadow of the same chest where we used to leave notes for each other when we were children. Its bright white colour glowed in the early light, so different from the yellowed envelopes of Grandad's old letters.

My stomach dropped at the sight of it, as though I already knew what weight it held. I think I knew from the moment I opened my eyes and found him gone. But still I scrambled to unravel it, because that is the thing about love: in your mind, you know the truth, you know what will come will hurt you, but there's always that hope that this time it just might be different, that you'll get your happy ending.

I smoothed the paper out against my knee. Two words in his handwriting – I would know it anywhere, all those cramped joined-up letters with never quite enough space for the apostrophe. Two words, and nothing else.

I'm sorry

CHAPTER 1

Now

Though it follows all of the same seasons as home, the countryside never changes. It hides beneath a blanket of snow in the winter, scorches under the sun in the summer, and blooms in a rainbow in the spring. But still, there's something constant about it, as though it stays still as the world around it bends, twists, and breaks.

At least, that's what I used to think. Every summer for almost ten years, we'd visit Granny and Grandad on their farm to spend our time out in the fields, filling our lungs with enough fresh air to flush out all of the smog of London.

As Mum drives, I see the apple tree that grew the fruit that Callum lost his tooth into when we were eight, and the gaps in the wheat fields that were tracks for races I always lost. We pass by the streams where we caught fish with our little makeshift nets. But the childish wonder of staring out the window and dreaming of what adventures lay ahead hasn't quite hit me the same this time around.

Callum sits beside me, his headphones stuffed into his ears so he doesn't have to listen to mum's podcast on the aux. I tuned it out two hours ago, but now the dull vocal fry of the host discussing 'how to beat corporate burnout' is starting to grate on me. Plucking a headphone from Callum, I pop it in my ear and his audiobook on the Tudor dynasty is quickly paused and swapped out for our shared playlist with an eye roll.

'Ugh, skip this one,' I mumble about the next four songs.

On the fifth, my brother snaps back. 'You're really annoying, you know that.' He shakes his head. 'Every one of those songs was one *you* added.'

They were all songs played at Granny's funeral, but Callum doesn't make the connection, and I don't tell him either. Instead, I stick out my tongue and tell him to skip the next one. He doesn't protest, nor does he shake me off when I lay my head on his shoulder.

It's been two years since I've been back in this part of the country. Two years since Granny died, two years since Jacob Thorogood broke my heart, and two years since my life felt truly whole.

The landscape hasn't changed, no. But everything is different.

Callum tried to convince me to come back with him last summer. He's better at dealing with things than me. He's a 'grab the bull by the horns' kind of guy, but despite being his twin in every other sense of the word, this is where I am his opposite. I didn't return last year.

This year, I have no choice.

When the car stops, Callum hops out of the car with the same excitement as always. Arriving at the farm always felt like Christmas when Granny was alive, but now I can't bring myself to follow him.

'Ava?' Mum turns to me from the front seat. 'We're here . . .' She says it as though I was too away with the fairies to notice.

She has a nervous smile on her face, the same one she's had for the last few weeks as we've slowly packed our home into boxes and left a life behind. It's her 'brave face'. She wore the same one at Granny's funeral, as though she believes that letting her smile drop for even a second would make everyone else spontaneously burst into tears.

I don't reply, only sit stubbornly in the back, my arms folded like a toddler on the verge of a tantrum. Mum sighs. She does that a lot these days.

'Come on, Ava. You can't just sit here. We need to start unloading.' Mum's patience is wearing thin. She was the same back at home, packing boxes as though it was nothing, growing more annoyed as I stared at my empty cardboard, trying not to cry.

If I get out now, that will make all of this real. As soon as I put my shoes onto the gravel of Grandad's driveway, it will all hit me: that we left Dad behind in London, that our lives have to start over again, that this place of summer holidays is now our new home.

'I know this isn't what you wanted, Ava, but I've told you why it is the way it is. Your dad's job is too demanding to look after you and your brother, and now that I've quit mine, I can't afford for us to stay in London. I know it's not ideal . . . but that's how it's going to be.'

She used to be some high-up exec in some fancy company with an office in a building with too many floors. I imagine she had to be ruthless there too, smashing all the glass ceilings and whatnot, but Mum and Dad's divorce doesn't feel like business to me – it's not like a dissolution of a contract with no emotions. Everything I have ever known is being tossed in the blades of a combine, and I'm just supposed to collect the scraps as if nothing has happened.

Mum is good at switching off her feelings. She's always been the tough one, as though she's afraid to show any weakness. Maybe that's why we have never been close; I have too much heart, while she is all brain.

'I can't do it,' I say weakly. 'I can't just start again.'

'Well, you have no other choice, Ava. None of us have a choice.' She huffs. 'This is our fresh start.'

You had a choice, I want to scream at her. *Could you not have just got on for one more year? Let me finish school? Let me go to university? Not disrupt my life at its most important point? No, you were only thinking about yourself, weren't you.*

The words I long to say out loud get stuck before they can reach Mum, but they do enough damage in my mind to send angry tears running down my face. Sighing again, she turns away from the car for a moment before she spins back around to look at me with sad eyes. 'This was the right choice for our family, Ava. I hope one day you'll be able to see that.' And she strides away before I can fight back any more.

The only thing that pulls me out of my own head is my phone as it buzzes aggressively on my lap. Freya's name illuminates the screen, her little round profile picture glowing with her wide smile and bouncing coils of hair. It's from our photoshoot at college, where she agreed to model some of my designs as long as I promised to set her up with Ash in the year above. They've been together ever since, and I still like to take all of the credit for that.

Did you see him yet? 👀 x

Him. We both know who she's talking about: Jacob Thorogood. The boy who lives on the next farm over. The boy who has filled my summers my whole childhood. The boy that once felt like my whole world. But this time, I closed my eyes as we drove through the village, just so I'd have no chance of spotting him.

I reply:

Who?

Sweat pools in my palms at the thought of him and I slide my phone back into my pocket before she can reply. I don't want to think about him any more. I will myself to get out of the car and take my suitcase out of the boot.

Callum and Grandad are standing in the doorway when I reach them, discussing the weather from the last few weeks. Callum enquires about how 'his' chickens have been in the months without him.

'Hello Ava, love.' Grandad interrupts the conversation to address me. He isn't the hugging type, so he taps my arm with his swollen hands that are permanently stained with tractor engine oil. 'I was starting to worry that they'd left you behind.'

I smile, and this time it's genuine. No matter how I feel – about the divorce, about the move, about how much pain I feel standing here without Granny – Grandad always gets a smile from me. He's the only one I actually got in the car for.

'They couldn't keep me away,' I reply. We both know it's a lie. I kept myself away for two years, but it's enough to make Grandad tap me again on the arm and try his best to hide a grin.

Seeing this house – its red gables, its wisteria-covered brick work, and its assembly of roses lining the driveway –

was always the treasure at the end of what felt like an epic voyage when I was younger. Granny and Grandad would always be waiting at the door with smiles. As a kid, I always thought they had been standing out there all day just waiting for us to arrive. Granny would be wearing her apron and a silk scarf around her neck. Grandad would always have a tool or a knick-knack of some kind in hand that he was in the middle of tinkering with.

The roses have wilted early this year, and the flower beds are knotted with weeds. This was always Granny's patch. Whatever the weather, she'd be out here, kneeling on her little floral cushion, tending to her flowers as though they too were her grandchildren. Grandad had other, more important parts of the farm he needed to look after. Granny did too, but she always made time for her garden. We'd sit along here for hours, pruning, watering, admiring. Sometimes we'd talk, about school, about boys, the future, but other times, we were happy with the silence. Just knowing she was beside me, with the rhythmic slicing of the secateurs and her quiet humming, was more than enough.

'Now, I've made up your rooms,' Grandad says. 'But I couldn't remember which of you had which duvet cover, so for now, Ava you've got that Pepe Le Pig one.' He means Peppa Pig. 'Cal, you've got the one with them big bears on it.'

It's clear he's been struggling without Granny too, so I

don't mention that she bought us new ones five years ago, and neither does Callum.

'Thank you, Grandad.' I kiss the top of his head as I slide past him through the front door, dragging my suitcase behind me. I've grown a little in the last couple of years, and Grandad seems to have shrunk. Either that, or his shoulders are a little more slumped than the last time I saw him.

The inside of the house is similar to the outside. It's clear that Grandad has tried to keep up with all of the little things Granny did to make it homely. Her doilies are out on the sideboard, but they're dusty. The potted plants are just sticks in soil. And the photos lining the walls are perfectly straight, but covered in a thick layer of dust.

I park my suitcase in a corner, find the feather duster in the cupboard under the stairs and run it over a few of the frames and shelves. They're mostly family photos, and almost all of them have Dad in. The family seems to shrink every time I'm here. Seeing him in the photos, smiling away, I wonder what he's doing now. Sitting alone in our old house with the TV on low because now it echoes around the empty room? Thinking of a way to win Mum back and come and save his family? Or maybe nothing has changed for him at all. He'll be working, he won't be home until late, and it will be no different crawling into bed in an empty house than to a sleeping one.

Another picture makes me stop in my tracks: it's Jacob and me a few summers ago, back when I still had braces and he was still shorter than me. I have my arm slung around his neck, grinning at the camera, he's looking at me, his smile sneaking through, though he still tries to hide behind some of his fringe. We're both dressed in our best. That was always rare for him – you always knew it was something special when Jacob left his shorts at home and actually ran a comb through his feral mane.

Placing the feather duster back, I risk another peek at my phone. Freya has replied, and I can practically see her eyes rolling through her message.

Oh shush. Things might be different this time round x

Abandoning Mum and Callum to unload the rest of the car by themselves, I sneak through to the back door, unhook the latch and slip into the back garden. Sheds and timber frames of old barns are strewn across the landscape, but as I scramble over the few fallen beams and hop over one of the crumbling dry stone walls, I see it.

The old weeping willow still stands strong, with a trunk as wide as Callum, Jacob and me all standing shoulder to shoulder. Its branches curve over so low that the bottom leaves skim the floor, and behind the curtain of greenery lies the treehouse. It's exactly half way between Grandad's farm and Hope Farm next door and so much time has passed, I've forgotten who built it. It's been there so long that the willow's branches have begun to grow around the slats of wood, swallowing the joints of the structure so it's almost as if it grew like that, with a paned window and pointed roof.

Before I know it, I'm making my way there, driven by a forgotten sense of longing. There is no ladder to the treehouse, so I balance my way up the lowest branch, which bends down like an old gnarly limb reaching out to scoop you up. Once I'm inside, I realise it used to feel bigger. I can hardly stand inside it now; I have to crawl across the leaf-littered floor to not bump my head on the low ceiling. The interior of the treehouse is untouched. I suppose its usual residents don't visit much these days. None of us are children any more, and we're all too busy to play spies, or pirates, or knights and princesses. The wooden chest in the corner is unmoved, though a little weed has grown around it.

Instinctively, I move towards it, lifting the lid, and holding my breath as I check to see its contents. I can't help but hope there's a note for me here. Alas, nothing. Well, a family of woodlice have taken up residence in one of the corners, and there's an old wrapper from a cheese string, that was definitely left there by Callum, but no note.

Why would he leave one anyway?

I look around the rest of the treehouse. The photos wrapped in sandwich bags that were pinned to the wall are faded, and the printer ink has smeared so the faces are barely legible. We'd printed them at the library a few years ago, after stealing the rusty bikes from the shed and pedalling into town as fast as we could. We had to beg the librarian to let us use the computer. We did everything we could think of to protect the streaky sheet of A4 paper from the elements, though back then, all we could think of was the leftover plastic bag from Jacob's jam sandwiches that was still sticky on the inside. I don't need to see the photo now though. It's still so engrained in my mind.

It was Halloween. Both of us were in our matching costumes that no one understood but us. Jacob should have another copy somewhere, but knowing him, he lost it before he even made it home. And I doubt he would care for its sentiment now anyway.

A shiver runs through me at the memory of the last time I was here. The last time *we* were here; when he kissed me.

My body prickles at the thought as goosebumps cover my flesh. If I close my eyes now, I can almost feel him here, his hand wrapped in my hair, his lips mapping out my own with such urgency it was as if he had waited a lifetime for the opportunity. Though my heart pounds now, it didn't then. His touch had filled me with such peace, such tranquillity, that it felt like coming home to a love that would protect me for the rest of time. How wrong I was.

'Ava!' Mum's voice shouts across the back garden and snaps me out of my thoughts. 'Ava?'

Peeping my head out of the treehouse door, I see her frantically pacing. She visibly sighs when she sees me. 'Oh, there you are. What are you doing up there?' She doesn't give me chance to reply as she runs a stressed hand through her thinning hair. 'Come on in and get unpacked. The Thorogoods are coming for dinner.'

CHAPTER 2

Ten years ago

I first met the Thorogoods when I was eight years old. Bouncing out of the car, my blue glitter jelly sandals filled with tiny pebbles as I crash landed onto Granny and Grandad's front garden. I didn't even bother to shut the door as I rushed to Granny and buried my face into her skirts as she welcomed me with open arms. I just knew from her flour-covered apron that she'd been baking my favourite jam tarts. She always put little love hearts cut from the spare pastry on top. Nothing ever went to waste in her house, and she never made anything that didn't look like it was fresh out of a book of fairytales.

'Hello, little one.' She kissed my head.

'I've missed you.' My voice was muffled through the fabric of her skirt.

Granny laughed softly and pat me on the back. 'We've missed you more.' She pried my hands from around her legs and bent down so she could look me in the eye. 'Why don't you come on in? We've got your favourite tea on the table.'

I did as I was told. All of Granny's teas were my favourite teas, and there was always lots of pudding afterwards, smothered in custard, of course. Well, I loved everything at Granny and Grandad's house, especially the fields that seemingly stretched for miles and miles. Grandad always let me feed the sheep, and we were allowed to get as mucky as we'd like. In London, we only had one tiny park, where the foxes weren't too keen on being stroked and the tarmac wasn't as soft to fall on as the grass. Mum always moaned when I wore holes into the knees of my tights from crawling around, I'd scuff the toe of my shoes within moments of wearing them too. I understand her frustration now, but eight-year-old Ava was more concerned with turning over every stone and piece of litter to look for bugs and beasties.

When the unpacking was done, we all sat down at the kitchen table for Grandad to dish up the roast. Mum always stayed for the first night to let us settle in before she had to go back to London. It always made me giggle because it was like she was a kid here too: Granny warmed her pyjamas on the fire at the same time as mine and Callum's, Grandad always plated up dinner for her, and made her eat all of her carrots before she was allowed pudding. I always thought it would be nice if Mum could stay all summer, but she said work needed her and that Dad would be all by himself. She didn't want him to be lonely without her for too long.

'Anything new on the farm then, Dad?' Mum was asking, reluctantly plopping another carrot in her mouth. I didn't know why she was always so fussy. The carrots were grown in Granny's garden and I always thought they tasted more orange and carrot-y than the ones we'd get at Tescos.

'Aye, lass,' Grandad replied with a mouth full of mashed potatoes.

'Care to share?' Mum laughed at him.

Granny rolled her eyes and answered for Grandad. 'We've got new neighbours, over the way at Hope Farm. Old Mr Dixon decided to sell up over the winter, and there's a new family in there now. What were they called again Harry?'

'Thorns? Thorolds? I dunno, but they have got a lovely John Deer and the fella said he'll let me have a go on it, but he 'ant been round yet that bloo—'

'—Thorogood, that's it!' Granny interrupted before he could continue. 'Mum, Dad, and their three boys. I'm pretty sure the middle one is the same age as you twins.'

'They've been out playing in that bit of land at the back, taken over that old treehouse. You know, that Dixon swore was his, but I could bet on my life that it was on our deeds, wasn't it, Dot?' Grandad grumbled, but he softened when Granny laid her wrinkly hand on top of his.

'They seem like good lads,' Granny said. 'I still need to have the family round for tea, give them all the gossip about the village; you know how it is, Pip.'

Mum nodded, but I was still hung up on the prospect of

new friends over the summer. Don't get me wrong, I loved the days where Granny was my best friend, but it would be nice to play with people who didn't just let me win every game we played, and who could last longer than five seconds at tig.

After dinner, once we'd finished the washing up, I tugged Callum by his shirt sleeves. 'Come on!' The thought of new faces was still hot in my mind.

The July evening was still light and warm, so I left my coat and shoes behind. I sped across the garden, the grass tickling in between my toes with every step. Dodging around farm machinery, the outbuildings, and the chickens that had squeezed through their fence to pick at the worms, it felt like the rest of the world could be out here at the end of Granny's garden.

'Where are we going?' Callum finally asked as I slowed down to look out across the open fields. He was out of breath, but he would never say no to following me on an adventure.

Scanning the horizon, I pointed to the old willow tree in the distance. 'There.'

We jogged through the ploughed field and by the time we reached the tree, the mud reached my knees. I'd played in the treehouse before, but on that day it seemed different. The branches were pruned. The tree looked neat and tidy, and the wooden house sitting in the middle of it looked alive. A skull and cross bones had been drawn onto an old pillowcase and flew like a flag from one branch. Chalk sketches decorated the walls like cave paintings depicting stories of castles, beasts and bravery.

'Wow,' Callum breathed as he looked at it with an open mouth. He said exactly what I was thinking as my legs trembled with excitement.

'Stay here and be my look out,' I ordered my brother. He saluted me with such conviction, I knew no one was getting past him.

Scaling the lowest branch, I hauled myself into the house. A sharp pain stung my foot as I snagged my sole on the raw wood with a hiss.

'I bet you've got a splinter now.' A quiet voice that I'd never heard before came from the corner. A boy about my age was lurking there, surrounded by piles of books and a collection of rocks and feathers.

I sat down cross-legged to inspect my toe. The stranger was right. A thick splinter was jutting out from the filth of my big toe and I winced at the sight of it.

'Who are you?' I asked, pretending that my toe wasn't throbbing and the tears weren't threatening to fall.

'Who are you?' he parroted. His hair was scruffy and sticking up in so many different directions that I'd swear he was a scarecrow if he weren't talking to me. His feet looked like mine, though – shoes of mud enveloped them.

'I asked you first.' I folded my arms over my chest.

'You're in my treehouse.'

'Well, my grandad said that this is his field. So, this is *his* treehouse.'

'So, you're Farmer Harry's granddaughter then?' He smiled as if he'd caught me out. 'I'm Jacob.' He got up from his shadowy corner and stretched out an equally dirty hand to shake as he came to sit beside me.

'I'm Ava.' I squeezed my foot, hoping that stopping any blood flow to it would also stop the tingling pain of my splinter. I didn't want this boy to think I was a baby.

Jacob grabbed something from one of the chests and opened it on his lap. 'Bug collecting kit,' he said, as though he could see me watching him closely.

'Cool.'

'Here, give me your foot.' He took a pair of tweezers from the kit and I couldn't hide the way my eyebrows climbed my face. Going to the doctor was always scary, and this felt all too similar. 'Don't worry.' Jacob pressed the ends of the tweezers together and they clicked softly. 'They're only plastic. It will hurt more if you leave it in. My brother left one in his thumb and it got all big and yellow and then it started leaking all of this smelly stuff. It was gross.'

Cautiously, I extended my foot out towards him. He gripped my ankle gently, though just firmly enough that I couldn't squirm away. Like a surgeon, Jacob took his plastic tweezers, positioned them over my splinter and plucked it out in one swift motion.

'Ow!' I squealed.

'Ava?' Callum's panicked voice called from outside. 'What is it? Did the baddies get you?'

I peered out the 'door' – more of a hatch in one corner of the treehouse – and found my twin halfway up the same branch I had just used, gripping onto it for dear life.

'I'm okay, just a splinter,' I shouted back. 'Here, take my hand.' I reached out and dragged him up into the treehouse. 'This is Jacob—' But when I turned back to introduce Callum to my new friend, he was gone.

Rushing to the window, I found a rope ladder swinging from its frame. Jacob was nowhere to be seen. Looking back now, I know he ran because he was shy, but back then it felt like I was going crazy. I spent far too long questioning whether he was even real at all. When we were kids, Jacob hated being in a room of more than a few people, he didn't like having to make conversation, or pretending to listen. I'm sure he'd have run away from me too if I had been any slower climbing that tree, but perhaps it was fate that he stayed.

'Oh,' I said, though Callum didn't seem to notice.

'Woah, cool!' He was too busy rooting through lunchboxes filled with chalk and chests filled with all kinds of treasure – trinkets, action figures, seashells and whatever else.

Grabbing a pencil and a notebook from one of the chests, I scrawled a note and hoped that if Jacob was real, he would read it on his next visit.

Thank you

Callum came up behind me, sporting a knight's helmet, a stick in place of a sword, and a hobby horse thrust between his legs. 'You're writing them a note?' he asked.

I nodded.

'Ask if we can join their club. I can be a knight and you could be a pirate!'

So, I did just that. My handwriting had never been the neatest and it looked particularly scratchy as I pressed the page against the woodgrain as a makeshift table. I signed it off with a questionable drawing of two crossed swords before looking about for somewhere to leave it that wouldn't get wet, or blown away. Finally, I found a nail by the window that wasn't hammered fully into the plank and pierced the page with the blunt end. Our note flapped against the treehouse like an old WANTED poster.

Clambering down again, and helping Callum, I took one last look in the direction of Hope Farm, trying to catch a glimpse of the mysterious, muddy boy in the distance. The only thing that moved seemed to be the clouds as they floated on with the wind. It was then that I started to wonder if I'd dreamt the whole thing. Could 'Jacob' have been the ghost of a knight haunting his old castle?

CHAPTER 3

Now

'The Thorogoods are coming for dinner.' For the last ten years, that's been a completely normal sentence in this house. So why does it now fill me with feelings I can't quite explain?

The boys and their parents have become our extended family over the years. Hope Farm is home just as much as this place is – there's no need to knock on the door, just letting yourself in to grab a plate of food and lounge on the sofa is standard practise in both houses. Never once have I felt out of place in the Thorogood family, so why did I have to ruin it all by kissing the one that meant the most?

Now back on the farm and with dinner prepped, I look out at the treehouse from the confines of my Peppa Pig bedding, counting down the minutes until their arrival. Never have I been this nervous about seeing Jacob. In fact, he was always the one person that just seemed to understand me, as though we are cut from the same cloth, sharing one soul. From the very moment we met, I felt safe with him. He was like another home, just as much as these walls with Granny and Grandad, this stupid childish bedding, and that higgledy-piggledy treehouse at the end of the garden. That's why he was the only one I could talk to, the only one who could comfort me after Granny's death. Even Callum, who is a mirror image of my own DNA, couldn't get close back then.

Back before things got awkward, I'd have already been out to find him by now. We'd hide under a blanket in the treehouse and I'd tell him all about Mum and Dad. Tell him that I am afraid of the future, of love, of grief. But things are so different now. The thought of seeing him only adds to my anxiety. The constant nausea I've felt since Mum and Dad sat me down to tell me they're divorcing only grows at the prospect of him walking into this house.

How am I meant to sit across from him at dinner and act like it's all okay?

The doorbell ringing forces me out of my thoughts. Sweeping away a stray tear, I straighten out my outfit as if it's something fancier than just jeans and a t-shirt. Normally, my outfits are the sunshine, even when I don't quite feel so sunny myself. Always drenched in colour, always layered with florals. But I can't bring myself to wear anything happy today. Not in this house, not without Granny here.

I creep quietly down the stairs. My attempts to go undetected are futile as the Thorogood clan gathers in the hallway, each taking off their boots and wellies, their voices overlapping in various conversations.

'Ava!' Alfie, the youngest brother, spots me first and makes sure that no one else can be ignorant of my presence. I can't help but smile at him. He must be seventeen now, a tall bunch of gangly limbs and a smile so lopsided, it's impossible not to mimic him.

'Hi Alf, how are you?' Too impatient to let me reach them properly, he lifts me off the bottom step in a big hug, no doubt showing off his new muscles that have piled on since I last saw him, and I slap him on the shoulder to set me back down. 'Been in any trouble recently?'

'Only the same old stuff. That college don't appreciate budding entrepreneurs.' He huffs. 'I got suspended for a couple of days for setting up a car wash in the car park. It's not my fault they're missing a trick! Could be making loads.'

'What he's not telling you, Ava, is that he did it *only* in his pants.' Will butts in and offers out his hand for me to shake. He's never been a hugger. He's the oldest and most serious. Will Thorogood was always King Arthur when we were kids – the boss. Callum and I didn't mind, but his brothers and Lizzie, the Thorogood cousin, were always desperate to usurp him for power.

'You alright, Will?' Seeing the two brothers' faces softens a little of the storm in my stomach.

'You know me, always just right. How are you, Matthews?

We've brought you your favourite.' He hands me a dish filled with Mrs Thorogood's famous lasagne and I accept it with a grin.

'I'm much better at the sight of this. Thanks, Sian.' I raise my voice just a little so the parents can hear me from behind their sons. I catch Mrs Thorogood's eye and thank her with a wink.

There is one face I don't see within the family, which is strange, because I always seem to find his face first in a crowd, as though my body has a homing beacon attached to him, and vice versa. No matter what, we could always find each other.

Once, we got separated foraging in the woods on the edge of the Wolds. I still have no idea how Jacob managed to find me the moment the panic began to set in. I was sure my time had come. It must have been less than half an hour, but already I was panicking about having to eat worms and drink from a brook, but before I could stoop too low, Jacob emerged from the trees, sweaty from running. He swept away my tears with his muddy hands, the held my hand the whole way home, just to be sure he wouldn't lose me again.

'Looking for Jake?' Will asks slowly. I shake my head, but my red cheeks probably give me away instantly. 'He's not here. He's . . . ill. Won't stop throwing up. Sends his love though.'

'I thought he was at the pub,' Alfie juts in. Then he turns

to me conspiratorially. 'As soon as he turned eighteen, he's pretty much started squatting in there. Still won't sneak me a pint into the beer garden though.'

'Come on in, come on in.' Mum emerges from somewhere further inside the house and begins to shepherd the neighbours into the kitchen. I'm grateful for the distraction before the boys can notice how my smile has evaporated at the mention of Jacob. My stomach sinks and each step as I follow behind them feels heavier than the last.

Ironic, isn't it? I was dreading seeing him, and here I am, achingly disappointed by his absence.

'Oh, Pippa, how are you, duck?' Sian asks as she sees Mum. 'We thought you might appreciate some company.' My hearts pangs once again. What about Dad? What about his company? He loved Sian's lasagne too. He would always make sure to text Dave Thorogood ahead of time to warn them when he was coming up, just to make sure he'd dropped enough hints for her to make one specially.

Will and Alfie find Callum at the dining table, and they go through their typical boyish greeting of roughing each other up a bit – nothing says I've missed you more than minor aggression.

'Oh here, Sian, love,' Grandad says as everyone funnels into the kitchen. 'I've got all your dishes from last week.' He swaps out the trays of fresh food for empty ones that he's washed.

It's nice to know that he's had someone looking out for him. Granny meant a lot to everyone in the village, so it doesn't surprise me that they've rallied around Grandad since she's been gone.

This kitchen is the heart of the farmhouse; the Aga warms the whole thing through the winter, and no matter what the occasion, we all gather around the table that always has enough places to sit, even if we have to fashion more chairs out of garden furniture and old apple crates. I've never seen anyone turned away from this table – even the postman has popped in a few times for tea and cake. The surface is scarred with years of wear, the wood marked and stained from meals past, but to me it looks more perfect than if it was new. Somewhere near the head of the table, there's pencil marks from my year five homework. I must have gotten a little too carried away and ended up shading the table as well as the paper, but Granny never fussed, she just tutted, shook her head and accepted that that was now part of her kitchen. To me, this table represents all Granny stood for; her home would welcome anyone with a hot meal and pleasant company.

We all take our places at the table, and the seat beside me is empty. These big inter-family dinners were a regular thing in the summers – we all had our own set places, and assigned jobs to do in the clean-up. Jacob was always beside me, and we'd be tasked with taking the leftovers out to the pigs.

Losing myself in the memory, I tune out the voices that fill the room as dinner is dished out. It's only when I hear my name being called that I snap back into reality.

'How are you getting on, Ava?' Dave asks as he tucks into his place. 'You know what you're wanting to do after college yet?'

'I've, er, been applying to universities to study fashion. I do – er, did – a course in it at college, back home.' The thought of swapping colleges and starting all over again makes me feel sick. There is no fashion course offered at my new college, and I haven't quite come to terms with the fact that I'm going to have to finish off the whole qualification by myself, with my tutor hundreds of miles away and only accessible by email. I shove a fork full of pasta into my mouth before I can think about it too much.

I never expected to start a new school at eighteen. I certainly didn't expect to start a new school, in a new town, taking completely different subjects because my Mum and Dad don't love each other any more.

'Fashion, eh?' Dave replies. 'That's out there. You kids these days go to university for anything. Back in my day, you left school at fifteen and went to work with your old man or his mate.'

I laugh along to be polite. It's the same sort of spiel I've heard from plenty of other people's dads that are still stuck in the 1980s, including my own. He works in business, the same as Mum. Both of them view the arts as a hobby, something fun to do after you've finished your 'real work'. I still don't think that they're convinced I could make a career out of this, no matter how many PowerPoint presentations I've given them on my employment opportunities. It's okay; they'll see. I don't need to waste any energy on people who aren't actually that interested. I'm grateful when the topic shifts to Callum.

'You still collecting your mini figures?' Alfie asks. He loves to tease Callum about his nerdiness, but he's always the first one to want to have a look at his new collection.

'Yeah, but I had to leave a lot behind in London. Couldn't fit it all in the car, but brought enough models to keep me busy, and I couldn't part with my lightsabres.'

'I think we'd need a whole moving van just for his replica swords. Thankfully his dad was more than happy to keep hold of them for a while,' Mum adds, seemingly unbothered by the fact that Callum's swords aren't the only thing left behind.

'I've got a new PC though. I'll show you and Lizzie once I get it unpacked.' He tricked Mum and Dad into buying him a top spec computer 'for his school work'. They had no idea that he'd actually use it for his late-night video game battles that he'd keep us all up shouting at.

'Where's your Jacob tonight?' Mum asks once her son has

finished another tangent about famous historical battles and how he has found ways to re-enact them on his PC through some game.

'He's si—' Alfie begins, but his dad beats him to it.

'—out with his lady friend, Prue?' Dave says with a mouthful.

'Pen,' Sian corrects him with any eyeroll. 'You see her nearly every day, Dave.'

'Aye that's it. Never at home that boy, always out and about.'

Will looks at me with a grimace, and Alfie shakes his head with a sigh.

I can feel all the blood drain from my face, and I have to grasp for my water to cool myself. My hand trembles a little as I lift the glass to my lips. I don't know why I'm so surprised. I follow enough of their mutual friends on Instagram to have seen plenty of them in the background of photos. Jacob and Pen have been a thing for a while. Even before I left here the last time, they had something going on, and Jacob isn't the sort of person to do anything by half, so of course they're still dating. I've met her a few times – she's always been a friend of the family, to everyone really. She goes to college with him, they both listen to music I've never heard of, and she has an eyebrow piercing. Of course he's still with her. He'd be a fool not to be.

I put a hand to my mouth to stifle a gag. I can't seem to control it. My stomach doesn't feel too happy either. It's like when Mum and Dad first told me about the divorce – I could do nothing but dry heave for twenty minutes while sweating profusely.

'You okay, Ava?' Mum asks.

I nod, trying to swallow down my feelings.

'You look awfully pale, duckie,' Sian adds and now all of the eyes around the table rest on me.

'I–I'm just a bit warm, I think,' I reply, suppressing another gag. 'I'm just going to get some air.'

Heading to the back door, I don't bother to put my shoes on as I wander out into the garden and sit down in the earth beside Granny's wilted roses. Jacob and I have never been anything, I remind myself. He owes me no loyalty after a stupid kiss, especially after disappearing on me right afterwards.

I just wish he'd have come over to say hi. He was once my best friend, after all.

CHAPTER 4

Ten years ago

Jacob and I seemed to pick each other out of the group almost immediately. Even back then, we clicked right away. It was as if we'd known each other in a past life and finally had the chance to catch up on lost time – we understood one another from the get go.

Mum always went back to London the day after dropping us off, and that's when Granny and Grandad's true spoiling began. We had a second breakfast of pastries and hot chocolate as soon as her car left the driveway, and we didn't have to change out of our pyjamas if we didn't want to. Usually, this was the start of a carefree summer. But that day, I was jittery in my seat, desperate to head back to the treehouse and see if Jacob had seen my note.

'Do you think they got our note?' Callum leaned across the table with his mouth smeared in chocolate spread.

'Give them time,' I said, though my knee bounced under the table, rattling the silverware. 'It's only nine. I bet they haven't even got out of bed yet.'

Once breakfast was done for the second time, I couldn't mask my anticipation. Thumping up the stairs to my room,

I tore through my suitcase looking for some clothes I could wear to play in. Just as I dragged a t-shirt over my head, the sound of a horn startled me into banging my head against the bedframe. Leaping to my feet, I looked out of the window for the source of the noise, rubbing the pain out of the lump forming on my head.

There, at varying heights of the willow tree in the back field, were three boys. Jacob was sitting in the highest branch he could reach. I *knew* he wasn't a ghost! One of his brothers hung out of the window of the treehouse, a plastic cone still pressed to his lips like a trumpet. The smallest boy stood at the roots, waving ferociously.

'Callum!' I shouted as I flew down the stairs. 'They got our note! Come on, let's go!'

My brother stumbled through the kitchen, dragging on his trainers, not bothering to lace them as he followed me out the door.

'Make sure you're back for your dinner!' I heard Granny call after us.

'We will!' Callum replied, still with his mouth full, still wearing his Spider-Man pyjama top.

We raced out the back garden, my anticipation so potent that I could feel my legs wobble under me as I ran.

'Welcome to Fort Thorogood,' the trumpeter announced as we arrived. He was an older version of Jacob, though this brother's dark hair wasn't so wild, and he had no mud smeared across his cheeks. 'I am King William. This is Sir Alfred.' He pointed to the smallest brother in front of us. He had a long stick, almost as tall as him, that he was holding like a spear. Clearly, he'd been tasked to guard the fort, but I reckoned I could beat him in a fight if I had to.

'Alfred' folded his arms over his chest with a huff. 'It's Alfie,' he corrected. Then he addressed Callum with wide eyes. 'Cool shirt.' Callum's cheeks flushed red, and the excitement at the prospect of three new boys to play with was evident on his face. I wasn't too sure yet – was I really going to have to spend the whole summer as the only girl? It didn't bother me much, I knew I could keep up with them, but I worried that the boys might not think the same and I'd end up side-lined, as I often did with some of Callum's friends back home.

'You remembered your shoes today,' Jacob said gruffly from his branch. He was wearing shorts, his scabby and grazed knees out on full display, and already his shins were splattered with mud.

'I didn't forget them yesterday. I just didn't want to wear them,' I retorted. The truth was, Granny made sure I was wearing shoes that day, after she'd slathered my foot with cream and given me a new plaster.

Jacob raised his eyebrows in surprise.

'I see you've already met Sir Jacob,' William called down.

'Now, I have been informed that we had a couple of intruders here at Fort Thorogood yesterday. They left behind this bit of evidence.' He held up my note that had been torn from the nail before tossing it from the parapet where it floated down like a falling leaf. 'You wish to be Knights of my realm, eh, trespassers?'

I folded my arms over my chest in defiance. 'We weren't trespassing!'

But my brother wasn't so confident, and he said at the same time: 'Um, yes, please!'

William paused for a minute, and looked back into the treehouse like he was consulting someone. After a moment, his head popped back out of the window with a grin. 'Well, to become my Knights, you must carry out a series of tasks and challenges set to test you.'

'You take this a bit seriously, don't you?' I asked as I saw Callum's eyes widen again.

'Look, you wanna play with us or not?' William said, putting aside his kingly voice.

I shrugged. 'Depends.'

'Depends on what?'

I shrugged again, much to William's annoyance. Jacob almost cracked a smile.

'I want to play! What's the first task?' Callum said, eagerness overtaking his anxiety briefly.

William ducked back inside for a second. When he came out, he said, 'You must battle one of my knights . . . to the death!' He dragged a stick from where it was tucked into his belt and thrust it through the window of the treehouse. He hesitated for a moment and murmured into the treehouse, 'Are you sure? To the death feels a bit dramatic.'

'Dramatic?' A new voice reached us as a girl shoved Will out of the way of the window, a helmet covering her hair as she waved her own 'sword' toward us. 'If you aren't cut out to be King, William, then I shall have to find someone else.' She pointed her stick towards Callum, who practically vibrated with excitement. She dropped the act for just a moment to stare down her cousin. 'You know Auntie Sian will tell you off if you're not playing with me.'

Will harrumphed and dropped the stick before sliding down the branch to meet us on the ground. 'You always ruin the fun,' he grumbled, as though being scolded by his mum, despite the fact that the girl looked like the youngest of all of us here. She followed him down.

'I'm Lizzie, or Sir Elizabeth. Their cousin and your challenger.'

I shook Lizzie's outstretched hand.

'Ava.' I smiled, excited at the prospect of having at least one other girl to play with. 'This is my brother, Callum.' He smiled too and offered a hand, but they both had a little awkward dance as they tried to figure out which hands to shake.

'Ignore Will,' she declared. 'He's nearly ten and thinks that makes him the boss. But I'm seven, and I actually am the boss. Nice to meet you.' I liked her already. Will cowered moodily by the trunk. Callum could only stare at her in awe.

'Come on, we need to do something, Liz. I'm bored,' Alfie moaned, and a sly smile crossed her face.

'Well, I didn't come all the way down here just to make friends. I came . . . for a *duel*!' Lizzie turned to me first but she was met with my wide eyes and shaking head. Without missing a beat, she turned to Callum, her eyebrow raised, 'You, Sir! Will you have the gall to fight for the crown, or die trying?'

Callum nodded his head so enthusiastically you'd have thought she'd just asked him to swim in a chocolate river, or pet a new-born puppy. I couldn't believe we were actually twins in that moment.

But I watched as Callum and Sir Elizabeth jabbed their sticks at each other, getting further and further away from the willow in their excitement. Every time Callum would get a little too close, he'd mumble an apology quickly, before Lizzie would use his moment of chivalric hesitation to strike harder and faster than before. With every clash of branch, I cringed, waiting for it all to be over.

That was, until Jacob climbed down from his perch to stand beside me.

'Thank you, by the way,' I said to him.

'You already said that.' When he saw my confused expression, he clarified, 'In your letter.'

'Well, my toe is much better.' An awkwardness settled over us for a second.

'You don't want to join the joust?' he asked.

'Don't you?'

He shrugged. He was standing closer to me now and I could see each freckle that decorated his nose and cheeks.

'Why have you already got mud on your face?' I asked, leaning forward to rub it off, like Granny did to me when we stood at the sink washing our hands before teatime.

Jacob dodged my fingers. 'Why don't you already have mud on your face?' He smiled properly now, his eyes nearly disappearing behind the creases of his skin.

He bolted behind the curtain of willow leaves, re-emerging a moment later with both hands caked in soil as though he'd just washed them in a mole hill. He paced towards me slowly, intention clear on his smirking face.

'Don't you dare.' I narrowed my eyes at him, suspiciously backing away.

'What?' His face softened into a look of innocence, but still he continued walking towards me, one slow step at a time. 'You know . . . a lot of animals use mud as a sort of sun cream. Our pigs splash in the mud every summer. It keeps them cool.' He rubbed his hands together conspiratorially, folding the mud over his palms until it clung together in one great glob.

Dodging away from him, I attempted to hide behind the thickest part of the trunk, but we paced around it, stalking each other like predator and prey, the threat of muddy t-shirts looming. Deciding I wasn't going to be the first to fall, I scooped up a fistful of mud, feeling it slot under my nails, and tossed it around the tree. I missed, but it splattered across his feet as it hit the ground.

'That's it!' He laughed as he chased me around the trunk. I screamed and ran, but he was faster, and soon he had one of my arms in his grip. He hugged me close as I wriggled to try and free myself. When he finally held me still, I squeezed my eyes close and prepared for defeat, expecting a big splatter of mud everywhere.

Instead, a soft hand presses against my cheek, and a cold smudge covered my face as he branded me softly with a muddy handprint. When I opened my eyes again, he had released me to take a step back and admire his work.

'Go on, then,' Jacob said, gesturing to his face. 'My turn.' He pushed his chin out before me and I smeared my own muddy hand on his opposite cheek. 'Now we have our own secret group.' He grinned, caked in soil, before running back to the stick fight. I followed him, hoping my brother hadn't been impaled, my face so warm I could feel the mud of his print drying out and cracking already.

By the time we reached the others, the 'fight to the death' had been resolved. Callum had lost, but because he put up such worthy fight, King William had accepted him as a knight for his bravery.

'To the swing?' Jacob suggested, not letting any more knightly squabbles test whether or not I could join.

'Race you there!' Alfie screamed, already running towards a treeline.

We all ran, and by the time we reached the edge of a stream, it didn't matter who had won. Will and Lizzie were arguing between themselves while Callum watched on, amused, and Alfie was kicking at the grass, already bored. Lizzie held a knot of rope in her hands that she kept pushing towards her eldest cousin.

'Go on. You go first, you're the biggest,' she said.

Will pushed her hand away. 'You're the champion knight, so you should go first.'

I surveyed the rope from afar. It was tied around a thick branch that reached over the stream. I was pretty sure I could leap across with a good enough run up.

'How about guests first?' Lizzie turned to Cal, who

flushed once again.

'Absolutely not,' he declared.

'Jake?' Will addressed his brother, who eyed me nervously before reluctantly reaching for the rope.

'You bunch of babies!' I pushed him aside and grabbed it myself. 'Clear out!' I said, and everyone shuffled aside to give me a path. When I was far enough away from the stream, I held on tight, ran, and sprang onto the rope.

I swang across the stream, once, twice, three times—

'Erm, I think you should have let go by now,' Alfie called, finally paying attention.

Realising that I no longer had enough momentum to reach the other side, I plunged down into the muddy bed. Cold but giggling, I emerged from the water, dripping like a swamp monster, surrounded by the sound of rapturous laughter from my new friends.

CHAPTER 5

Now

'Where are you off to so early?' I call.

Grandad jumps at the sound of my voice. I sit in the dark at the kitchen table, where I have been for the last hour or so, unable to sleep, or even to rest. I tried listening to Freya's ten-minute voice note about how her week has been, but I couldn't focus after the fourth minute. I'm not sure if it's being back here without Granny, or the thoughts of Jacob playing on my mind, but it felt easier to sit down here with a cup of tea than to keep tossing and turning in bed.

'Christ, you scared me. Could've given me a heart attack.' Grandad clutches his chest with one hand whilst he holds his boots in the other.

'Sorry,' I say, getting up to flick on the kettle again.

'Couldn't sleep either?' Grandad asks, as he steals my seat to pull on his shoes, not looking at me as he ties his laces.

I hum in response and we both fall quiet to the sound of the bubbling kettle. When it reaches boiling, I take a mug and pour him a cup. He accepts it with a smile that doesn't quite trigger the deep wrinkles that he's earned after decades of laughter.

'Look at him smiling out on that tractor, eh?' Granny used to say as we'd watch him as he'd weave up and down the east field, his grin so broad we could see it all the way back at the kitchen window. 'Nothing this man loves more than farming.' She'd shake her head with a laugh.

I know that's not true. Even when I was fifteen, I knew it. I saw the way Grandad looked at her from across the dinner table, or when he'd wave to her from leagues away, making sure he could always keep her in his sights. No, there was something Grandad loved more than farming: Granny.

'You make tea like your Granny. Strong and sweet. Just like the both of you,' Grandad says between swigs from his steaming mug. I don't think he realises how gut-wrenching his words are, or at least he doesn't want to acknowledge it. He just stares into his mug without looking at me for a moment, before he finally looks up. 'I'm off out on the tractor. You fancy a ride?'

'Yes, please.' I haven't felt the hum of a tractor under me for so long – the way it rattles my bones as we slice through the earth, or the unending bounce along the road until my coccyx is on fire. It doesn't sound so appealing put that way, but I've missed it.

'Come on then. Bring that packet of biscuits with you as well if you want.' He poses it like it's a choice, but Grandad doesn't play when it comes to his snacks. If he isn't covered in crumbs, he isn't happy.

So, with a packet of digestives in tow, I follow him out the back and wait patiently at the shed for him to strike up the tractor. It grumbles and coughs a little before kicking into life. It's an old bit of kit, but it's got him through plenty of harvests. There's nothing Grandad can't fix with a bit of duct tape and his unwavering tightfistedness. He would rather push the thing through the field than call a mechanic out, though I know Lizzie has lent him a hand on occasion.

When he manoeuvres it out of the barn doors, I close them behind him and hop up into the cab. There isn't quite enough room for two, so my thigh presses against the door painfully, but I don't protest.

'You were a bit smaller the last time you sat up here with your old man.' Grandad looks over to me as we chug through the yard. 'I remember the days I could get you, your brother, and a lame sheep in here all at once.' As we begin to trundle over the rough earth, I hit my head against a bar or two, but still, I only smile.

'Remember that time we found that goat out in the west field? I had to bear hug it the whole way home so it didn't leap out,' I reminisce. Grandad has a ghostly smile on his face.

'Aye. You've always been a strong old lass. I always remember you beating all the Thorogood boys at their arm wrestling. Dave told me their Will started going to the gym after you handed him his arse.'

'He always played the big man.' I chuckle at the memory. 'He's never underestimated me since, that's for certain. I don't think I'd be able to beat him now.'

'You'd still beat Alfie, I reckon.'

'Oh, without a doubt.' We settle into a comfortable silence as Grandad concentrates on the open land ahead of him. Tearing into the packet, I hand him a biscuit and we both crunch in tandem as the sun begins to peek from behind the horizon, bathing the wide sky in purples and oranges. The sunrises here are unlike any I've seen elsewhere. Without buildings, motorways, and a million commuters interrupting the wide expanses of land, the sunrise engulfs you. It's as though we're standing on the stone of a peach, surrounded entirely by its colours.

'How's things going with your sewing and bits?' Grandad asks as we watch the sky, making an attempt to talk about my escapades in fashion. He has as much knowledge of the subject that a seventy-year-old farmer who has worn the same woolly jumpers for three decades can possibly have.

'It's okay,' I reply, looking out of the window to avoid any eye contact. 'The college here doesn't offer fashion, so it's going to be a lot harder than it was back home.'

Grandad sighs audibly. 'I'm sorry, duckie.'

'Not your fault. Dave is probably right, though – the chances of me getting any sort of job in fashion now, especially now we're not in London, are pretty slim.' I haven't said any of these doubts out loud to anyone else. How can I tell Mum that the breakdown of her relationship is making me to miss out on my dream? I heard her crying last night in the bedroom beside mine, when she could finally drop her brave face.

That was one of the reasons I couldn't sleep. Sometimes, it's hard to tell that behind her business jargon and pantsuits, she's a real person, with real feelings. She tries so hard to make everyone believe she has it together all of the time, that she doesn't think maybe showing a little heart might be exactly what we all need. Maybe I should have gone in to her, hugged her and told her it was all okay, but I couldn't bring myself to. All I could do was listen to her sobs through the walls and stifle my own.

And what about Dad? Is he burying himself in his work like always? Or is he crying himself to sleep as well? Or – worst of all – does he even care? He's texted me a couple of times to check if we're settling in okay, but I can't bring myself to answer.

'Don't listen to Dave.' Grandad's voice interrupts the thought. 'All he knows is brussel sprouts and chicken feed. And he's got all boys.' He shakes his head and I find myself giggling at his jibe. 'I may be well past it, but I saw what you managed to do with your Granny's sewing machine. You have a special talent, and I know your Granny would hate you talking so pessimistic.'

It never gets easier hearing him mention her. The pain of losing her is still as raw as it was two years ago. Each one of his words sit heavy on my chest, as though just the memory of her can suck all of the life from me until the idea of ever being happy again feels completely out of reach.

Grandad, though his voice cracks at the mention of her, continues, 'And even if it does all go wrong – after you go away to your fancy school, if you don't have a job, or you realise you hate it – even then you'll always have a home at my farm. It may not be your dream, but you'll always have a place to belong, even after I'm long gone.' He takes his eyes off the track ahead for a moment to look at me with glassy eyes, and I know that no one has ever meant anything more in their life.

Unable to speak without the threat of tears falling, I rest my head on his shoulder like I did in this very tractor when I was younger, and he tenses a little at my touch before relaxing again into his seat.

'Anyway.' He says clearing his throat as though uncomfortable at his own soppiness. 'I have a load of trousers and bits for you to patch up for me, if you would? I went down the pub looking like I'd been in a fight with a hundred moths the other day.'

I sit back upright to answer him. 'Of course.' My fingers already itch at the thought of getting back to the sewing machine. It was always Granny that did his repairs, so whilst I revel in the honour of being asked, I can't help but feel that pang in my chest again knowing that she isn't here to do it any more.

'I never realised just how much your Granny did for me . . . everything feels like it's falling to bits these days.' His rare moment of candour breaks my heart a little more.

'Well, we're here now. You haven't got to worry about holes in your trousers any more.'

Before either one of us can be even more uncharacteristically mushy, Grandad pulls up to the orchard trees and kills the engine of the tractor. 'Gotta get these apples and pears in before the birds get to them,' he mumbles and we both hop out of the cab and harvest the fruit without another word.

Grandad doesn't work to the standard clock, or even the phases of the sun. No, for as long as I can remember, he has worked to the sound of his stomach. So, on its first grumble at 8:47 a.m., he sets downs his tools and announces that we must return home for breakfast.

Once all of the crates of apples and pears are filled and loaded into the trailer, we both climb back into the cab to head back to the farm. But with one cough, and a few grinding splutters, the tractor doesn't start.

'Don't worry, she does this sometimes.' Grandad persists for a few minutes, still insisting that a whack on the steering wheel and the flicking of a random buttons will make her kick back into life.

He only gives up hope when another audible growl of his stomach echoes around the cab. With a huff, he opens a little side compartment and picks up an ancient-looking phone. Several buttons have been taped off so he's in no danger of pressing the wrong ones.

'You know how to text?' I joke, though I'm still a little dumbfounded. I've never seen him use any technology more advanced than his microwave until now.

'Not really, but the boys at Hope Farm got me this phone last year so I can call for help if I get myself in a pickle.' The mention of 'the boys', and knowing who is included among them, makes me swallow hard, but I don't linger on the feeling too long. They've bought my grandad a phone. Granted, it looks as though it's been found in an archaeological dig, but that means they've been looking out for him.

A little guilt wedges itself between the warm feeling that thought brings. It should have been me here, helping him, keeping him afloat. Every year, he had Granny, Callum and me to help him, and yet, when he lost Granny, I neglected him too. Too clouded by my own grief, I never even stopped to think about the farm, or how Grandad would be working himself to the bone doing the work of the two that left him behind. I'm just glad that the Thorogoods are better people than I could even think to be.

Basking in the September sun, I climb out of the cab and sit at the bottom of the apple tree as Grandad hits various parts of the tractor with his cane, waiting for whoever he called a few moments ago.

Before he can do any more damage, a truck rumbles in the distance. 'About time,' Grandad grumbles as he walks up to meet his saviour.

The dark flat-bed pulls to a stop. The window rolls down and an arm leans over the door. 'What mess you got yourself into this time, Harry?' The voice is rough, deep, but just barely recognisable.

'Jacob?' I can't stop myself from springing to my feet to catch a glimpse of him for the first time in so long. I should act unbothered – cool, calm, collected – but something about him makes me throw all sense of 'should' out the window.

He looks almost the same – the same shaggy, messy hair, stained clothes, and deep dark eyes that are framed by freckles. And yet, he's grown. There's something distinctly masculine about him now, no trace of boyhood left on his face, with his jawline sharper than ever and splattered with a covering of stubble.

I thought my heart would race, or I'd go into a sweating frenzy at the sight of him. But strangely, I feel nothing but careful anticipation, almost as if all of the turmoil of expectation leading up to our meeting has melted away. It's like my body suddenly remembers that it's home.

Without missing a beat, he opens the door and comes to greet me at his full height. Now he well and truly towers over me in a frame that seems to have doubled since the last time we met. 'Kitty.' He says my old nickname so casually, as if pointing out a landmark on a long drive, and it knocks the wind out of me completely. No one has called me that for so long.

'I didn't know you could drive,' is the only thing I can think to say as I look up at him. All I see reflected is ten years of adventures with a friend, and I settle into a version of myself that feels more like *me*.

He watches me so closely, not once flinching away at the intensity of our meeting or even seeming ruffled by any memories. 'You've missed a lot.'

CHAPTER 6

Ten years ago

I still remember the day he gave me that nickname. It was the same day he got his. The first day we were all invited to Hope Farm for Sunday Dinner.

'Right, you two, straighten yourselves out.' Granny fussed around us in the kitchen. 'We've never been inside Hope Farm. You know how much of an old grump Mr Dixon was, and no matter how many times I hand delivered him some of our hen's eggs, he never so much as invited me in for a cuppa. Mr and Mrs Thorogood have been kind enough to ask us over, so the least we can do is look presentable.'

Granny licked her thumb and swiped it across a smudge of dirt left behind from another afternoon in the treehouse with Jacob. In those last couple of weeks, the mud had become my second-best friend, after Jacob of course.

Each day, Callum and I met the Thorogoods at the treehouse. Then Alfie, Will, Callum and Lizzie would disappear off into their battles and jousts, sometimes playing knights of the round table, other times pretending their sticks were light sabres, and Jacob and I would sneak away. We collected bugs from all around the farm to introduce to our bug hotel. We'd fashioned it together from bits of old wood from Grandad's shed. I didn't want to touch the worms at first – their lack of faces had always freaked me out – but Jacob was never scared of anything. He'd happily pick up any animal in need, whether a bird of prey, or a fox with a mean bite. He once had to rescue a badger from a trap, and her mode of thanks was to attack his ankles when he set her back down, but Jacob never even flinched, just understood that she was afraid and in pain, and simply shepherded her off into the woods. He was the bravest boy I knew, so I too, was learning to be brave. After a few days out with Jacob, I stopped crying every time I fell over, my knees were torn and scarred from hopping across streams, or crawling through brambles. I wasn't afraid to follow Jacob anywhere, and soon, I gained the courage to lead him too.

The walk from Granny and Grandad's to Hope farm wasn't too far, but since the road out the front had no pavement or streetlights to guide us, and Granny wasn't too stable on her feet, we had to take the longer route through the fields. Everyone else walked too slow for my liking, so I skipped on ahead, following the way I'd watched Jacob leave. Passing a row of trees and leaping over a dyke, I quickly found myself in the gardens of Hope Farm.

A pony grazed on the lawn, chewing on the long grass at the foot of a trampoline in the space that the lawnmower couldn't quite reach. Beside the flower bed, a trowel and a heap of soil lay as though forgotten in a hurry, along with various other garden tools dotted around the place. The Thorogoods must have been having a hard time trying to make their new house a home between running the farm and keeping track of their three children.

I'd never seen their farmhouse before then. Even from the back, it was a place of grandeur. Windows lined the brick on three different floors, their panes teasing a glimpse inside, and each room wore a different wallpaper that caught the evening sun in a rainbow of colour. Some of the old brick was crumbling, shadows of old climbing ivy still lingered around a few of the sills. It was clear that old Mr Dixon never gave it much attention. A little section of scaffolding was wrapped around the corner of the house, and at the very top board, a pair of spindly legs were swinging back and forth over the ledge, at the same height as some of Grandad's oldest apple trees.

Jacob noticed me at the bottom of the garden and waved from the top of his tower. He looked so natural at the same heights that made my stomach ache just thinking about, as though he was born to live in the wild like Tarzan or Mowgli, and he only lived like a normal boy to appease his family. Sliding down the scaffold with skill, he met me at the bottom, and though I never told him, I was glad he didn't expect me to climb up.

'Did you come by yourself?' he asked when he got close to me. I noticed the rips in his shorts and the grazes on his knees.

'No, they're just slow. When did you fall over?' I frowned at him. He was much more balanced on his feet than I was at that age, and his scarred knees even then were so tough it took a lot to tear the skin.

'There's a kitten that's been abandoned in the barn,' he started excitedly. 'And I was trying to catch it to feed it, but it was faster than me.' He shrugged as though the scratches were nothing.

'A kitten?' My concern for Jacob's injuries vanished at the mention of a furry friend in need.

'Yeah. One of the farm cats must have given birth and forgotten about it. I've been leaving food out for her, but I need to catch her to get a good look and make sure she's okay,' Jacob said casually.

'Can I see her?' I grasped him by the arm in anticipation. Jacob didn't answer me, only stared wide-eyed, and I realised maybe my tight grip on his forearm was cutting off a little of his circulation. 'Sorry,' I murmured, releasing him with hot cheeks. He was blushing too. 'It's just Mum and Dad say we can't have a cat in our house back in London,' I continued, 'but they're my absolute favourite. They're wild, grumpy, and so unbothered by people, unless they choose you. And if you're their person, it's like being the queen – you're the most special thing in the world. I'd love to be someone's special person like that.'

'You'd be lucky getting this one anywhere near you.' Jacob didn't look at me when he spoke. I reminded myself to not get too physical when I was excited. 'But I'll show you.'

I threw my arms around his neck and drew him into the tightest hug I could muster.

'Jacob? Are the neighbours here yet? Dinner's almost ready.' Jacob's mum's voice came from behind a screen door. It startled us both, and I pulled away quickly.

A beautiful woman emerged from the back door and spotted us. I'm sure now she was trying to contain her grin. Sian's dark hair was long, but swept away from her face in a pony tail. Jacob must have gotten his freckles from her, because they decorated her nose and cheeks like fairy dust. 'Oh, hello. You must be Ava.'

'Hello, Mrs Thorogood.' I felt like my whole skull was on fire, but she didn't seem to notice.

'Please, call me Sian. Are your granny and grandad on the way too?' At the mention of them, they rounded the corner of the hedge and came into sight with Callum in tow. 'Perfect, just in time. You kids come on in, and get your hands washed and ready for dinner.'

Even though dinner was at the top of my list of excitement

only minutes ago, I felt a little deflated. I hesitated for a moment, but started following her in.

Clearly, the disappointment was evident on my face, because Jacob leaned in close and whispered, 'Don't worry, we can sneak off after pudding. Mum always talks too much to notice that we're gone.'

So, with that promise, I strode into the Thorogood farmhouse with my heart on fire.

When all of the pleasantries were out of the way, we sat down for dinner. I didn't think I'd ever seen Jacob without dirt under his nails or his hair in his face, but, that night, he sat beside me, scrubbed within an inch of his life. Callum sat on the other side. Our plates were only placed in front of us less than five minutes ago, but already, the peas were the only things that remained on my brother's. Alfie had promised him a look at his stick sword collection in his bedroom after dinner, and I'm sure Callum had been too impatient to chew properly.

'You're lucky we have all three boys here tonight.' Mr Thorogood chuckled to himself. 'Getting all three of them in one room at once is a mammoth task these days.'

'Even just getting Jacob inside is the hardest task. I reckon I'd have better luck teaching the pony sign language most days,' Sian added.

Jacob only stared at his plate, and I felt his knee bounce on his chair beside me.

'I don't blame the lad,' Grandad said. 'Bit of fresh air in his lungs, there's no better place to be than outside.' He winked across the table at Jacob in support and my best friend lifted one corner of his lips in thanks.

'Harry has always been the same,' Granny added. 'Only comes home for feeding, just like one of the animals.'

'Exactly!' Sian swigged her glass of wine. 'Some days, I even have to wrestle clothes onto him.'

'Or hose him down in the garden when he comes home like *The Creature From the Black Lagoon*.' Mr Thorogood clapped Jacob on the shoulder with a wide palm. I realised then that Jacob never had much to say when there's a crowd of people. He was staying silent.

'He's like a dog,' Alfie said with a mouthful of mashed potatoes that padded out his cheeks like a hamster stocking up for hibernation.

The Thorogoods actually had a dog: a fat Labrador that moved so little when it was lying down that I had actually thought he was a rug when I walked in. Jacob wasn't anything like that.

'Maybe he's a wolf.' I shrugged. 'They don't need to wear clothes, or have baths. They have a double coat and the outer layer is waterproof.'

Jacob looked up from his plate with a grin. He was missing one of his front teeth and he poked his tongue in the gap.

'I like that,' he murmured, but only loud enough so I could hear.

Both of us were grateful when the topic of conversation shifted to Will and his upcoming year 6 SATs tests. Jacob finished his meal with a little glow in his face.

When all of the plates were cleared away and coffee had been offered to Granny and Grandad, Jacob and I finally had our opportunity to escape. We pulled on our wellies and I grabbed my jacket, but as always, Jacob braved the chill evening with bare arms and bare legs.

'You really are a wolf, aren't you?' I said as he led me. 'Adapt to any sort of climate, snowy, wet, or warm.'

He shook his head, but threw it back to howl into the night.

'Alright, Wolfie, my ears are ringing now.' I rubbed my left lobe with a smile.

When we reached the barn, he paused for a moment at the door. 'I'm telling you, she's fast. Even if you do get near her, I reckon she's a biter, or a scratcher at the very least. You sure you're ready?'

I nodded eagerly. If Jacob wasn't scared of grumpy badgers, I wasn't going to be scared of a tiny kitten. He slid the barn door open, but the insides were shrouded in darkness. Jacob wandered in as though he'd memorised the steps he needed to take. Reluctant to follow him, I waited for a moment, working up the courage and convincing myself that there are no monsters in barns – just a cute kitten. At the very worst, there could be rats, and I was sure the friend we'd come to see must have dealt with them already.

Jacob emerged from the darkness with two torches in hand, and passed one over to me. 'Come on,' he whispered. 'I can hear her near the grain.'

Following the path we marked out with our lights, we tiptoed around machinery and hay bales until Jacob silently gestured to the sack of grain in the corner. On top of it, a tiny tortoiseshell kitten was curled up into the folds. Its tiny belly, bloated from whatever Jacob had fed her earlier, rose and fell with each of her deep sleepy breaths.

Looking to Jacob, I could just about make out the features of his face in the glow of the torch. He was cracking a smile. I was sure my own face was a sight to behold. I couldn't decide whether to squeal or cry, so I did neither, and I could feel all the pent-up emotion burn on my cheeks as I widened my eyes and mouth.

Jacob gestured with his head for me to take a step forward. Approaching slowly, I held my breath, trying not to let even a single exhale disturb her. When I was within touching distance, I slowly reached for the little slither of chicken that I had stashed away in my pocket from dinner. Very carefully, I held it out towards her nose. The little pink button twitched once, twice, and then she peeled her eyes open. As soon as she spotted the meat, she set to work, chewing away as though she hadn't eaten for days. With one piece down, I fished out another, and another, until she was happy enough to let me stroke a single finger down her back. The fur rippled at my touch and I shivered with the contact. I looked back at Jacob with a mix of triumph and smugness, but he only watched on in wonder, as though he'd just watched me land a triple backflip off the top of the tractor.

Once all my chicken was spent, I sat down on the floor, a dusting of old wheat and grain under me. I could feel each scrap poking painfully, but I didn't care. I encouraged Jacob to sit down beside me, and he did exactly that. Still holding my breath, I waited, and waited, until the fabric of the grain sack we were leaning against crinkled, and a small sleek shadow leaped down. The cat crawled into my lap with a stretch and a purr.

'I think I'll call her Hope,' I whispered.

'Amazing,' Jacob breathed in a whisper, careful not to scare her away so soon. 'If I'm a wolf, then I'm sure you must be part-cat.' He hummed for a moment and then added quietly, 'Kitty.'

I couldn't hide my grin. I was someone's special person.

CHAPTER 7

Now

Words fail me as I'm face to face with Jacob for the first time since *that* night. So much has changed, and he's right. I have missed so much. Too much.

Though his presence feels like home, the man who shuffles around me now to take a look at the tractor might as well be a stranger. Completely unruffled by our meeting, he sets to fixing the tractor without another word to me. For a moment, I'm stunned. This is the same boy that would brave storms just to make sure he didn't miss a day with me in the treehouse. We would lie in the tracks of cabbage fields for hours just to have a moment where no one else could bother us. Now, he hardly smiles, hardly even looks at me.

I'm no longer the lone wolf's special person, the one person he lets in. No, I suppose he has Pen now. Jacob doesn't need me any more. So how do I tell him I need him now more than ever?

'Thanks, William.' Grandad claps him on the back and Jacob smiles, but doesn't correct him. Grandad has never been good with names. He calls me by Mum's name more often than not, or Granny's, though he hasn't done that for a while. I can't blame him when he mixes up the Thorogood boys when there's just about three years between the eldest and youngest.

'How long have you had this bit of kit, Harry?' Jacob asks as he lifts the bonnet and throws half his body over it.

'Oh, I don't know lad. Ten years? Maybe?' Grandad rubs at the stubble on his chin, trying to remember.

'Surely not. You had this hunk of junk when we moved to Hope Farm, and it was old even then.'

'Ah, yes. Probably twenty then, son.' Then he narrows his eyes. 'You watch what you say about my Betty. They used to build things to last, not like all the plastic crap they give you these days. No, she's got plenty of life in her yet.'

Jacob extracts a metallic piece that's almost unrecognisable from the rust. I can't even be sure if it's something that's supposed to stay in there or if it's meant to be pulled out. Grandad chunters to himself, then pretends to act busy as he runs his hands along Betty's body work.

With Grandad far enough away for his hearing aid to pick us up, I finally work up a little courage to speak again. 'How have you been?'

Jacob doesn't surface from the engine. 'Yeah alright.' His voice seems to echo around the machinery and he taps away at various parts.

'I was hoping I'd see you at dinner the other night.' I rock back and forth on my heels, my stomach growing more and more unsettled. Things have never been this awkward.

'I wasn't well.' He tosses a crumpled-up ball of duct tape onto the ground.

'Oh.' I hesitate. 'Your dad said you were with Pen.'

Jacob lifts his head so quickly that he smacks the back of it against the bonnet with a vibrating 'bonk' followed by a hiss of pain. He tries to play it off, but he reaches up and rubs his oil-covered hand across his crown.

'You're getting yourself filthy,' I mutter. 'Come here.'

He steps down from the tractor, and slumps down onto the ground as I comb my fingers through his hair, checking to see if he's already got a lump forming. 'You okay?' I ask him, trying to ignore my quickening pulse and my heating cheeks.

'When did you start getting bothered about being dirty?' His voice is gruff, and for the first time, there's a glimmer of acknowledgement of our past in his words.

I focus on the task at hand. 'There's no mark, no blood. You'll be fine,' I mumble, drawing myself away from him reluctantly.

We stare at each other for a moment. I can't read the expression on his face, and the feeling is alienating. I slump down beside him, and we sit in silence for a moment, with only the occasional ding from Grandad hitting various parts of the tractor.

'I'm happy for you, you know,' I venture. 'You're proper punching with Pen.' I nudge him in the shoulder like he's one of my mates. I'm telling the truth, too. I am happy for him, if he's happy. But it still feels hard to say.

'Yeah. Cheers.' He still won't look me in the eye. Instead, he runs his palms down his trousers repetitively, his leg bouncing slightly until his discomfort grows too much and he's forced to stand up and get back to work on the tractor. The more this interaction goes on, the more my comfort melts away, and the ache in my heart becomes impossible to ignore.

'We're still friends though, right?' I say, a little of my desperation slipping through. 'We'll always be friends?' If he hears me, he doesn't make any attempt to reply. He paces neurotically around the tractor, his hands rushing through his hair at such speed, I'm surprised none of the strands stay wrapped around his fingers. The pit in my stomach is a cavern now. 'Wolfie?' I urge.

The tractor kicks back to life with a loud grumble and he finally ceases his pacing. 'Yeah, friends.'

His words don't comfort me. Where is the Jacob that would tell me anything? The Jacob that wouldn't rest until he told me some new gnarly animal fact? The Jacob that held me as I cried after Granny's funeral?

'There she is,' Grandad says, rushing towards us with a

grin on his face. 'Told you she'd still work.'

'Harry, you really need to stop fixing your engine with duct tape, or your precious Betty will blow up one day.' Jacob shakes his head and wipes his oil-stained palms down his shorts.

Grandad looks a little guilty, then shrugs as he slams down the bonnet. 'Come and have some breakfast with us, lad. My thanks for fixing her up.'

Jacob begins to protest, but I beat him to it. 'Jacob is probably really busy with his own farm, Grandad.' He looks to me with a little dejection, but it doesn't linger long enough for me to fully decipher it.

'Nonsense, he's got half an hour for some toast. Come on, we'll race you.' Grandad doesn't hang around long enough for either of us to refuse. He hops back into his cab with the sprightliness of a much younger man.

'You don't have to come.' I loiter for a moment as Jacob collects his tools.

He points to Grandad, who is beckoning me through the window. 'I don't think Harry's going to let me get out of this one.' Jacob pauses for a moment and looks at me wholly for the first time since he arrived. 'I'll see you there.'

'Come on Ava, move your arse.' Grandad sticks his head out of the window to call to me, and I do exactly as I'm told.

The ride back to the farm is quiet. The only thing to listen to is the chug of the tractor and Grandad's stomach as it's grumbles grow louder with every passing minute. When home is in view, the sight of Jacob's parked truck implies that we very much lost the race. Old Betty may have life in her yet, but her speed is no match for her competitors that were actually made in this millennium.

Jacob and Will are sitting at the kitchen table with Mum and Cal, mugs of tea in front of each of them, with two spare.

'Oh 'ello Jacob.' Grandad claps Will on the shoulder as he moves to take his seat.

'So close.' The eldest brother teases.

'To what do we owe the pleasure?' Grandad continues, pretending not to hear him.

'You called me, Harry,' Will says. 'Although, I reckon from the scratchiness of the line, you've called me from the back pocked of your trousers. Just thought I'd pop over and check if you needed me anyway.'

'You two are such good lads.' Mum fusses around them as she starts dishing out toast and pastries. She'd never have this sort of breakfast on offer if we hadn't got guests, but I'm not complaining. 'Thanks for looking out for Dad. Who knows what trouble he could have got into if he didn't have you boys looking after him these last couple of years.' She shakes her head and I know she must be feeling the same guilt as I was back in the orchard.

'Well . . . we've been thinking,' Will begins. Jacob hardly raises his gaze from his plate so I linger by the sink, out of the way. 'We're all going to chip in to help you out on the farm, Harry. It's a lot of acres to cover as one man, and since we don't have too many winter crops, we have a bit of spare time.'

'Don't be silly. Your dad needs you boys.' Grandad shakes his head with a mouth stuffed full. 'I've managed this farm just fine with only my Dot by my side for longer than all of your ages combined.'

'But Mum isn't here any more, Dad,' Mum says gently. Then, with a bit more firmness, she adds, 'And you're not as young as you once were either. The twins and I will help as much as we can now we're back, but these boys know farming, they're strong, and they're hard workers.' Mum moves around to take Grandad by the hand. 'Let us help you, eh?' Callum nods, as though they'd planned all of this together.

As much as I want to agree, as much as I want to give Grandad everything I can, I can't help but sense fashion school slipping even further away. How will I have time to study my A-level independently if I spend all of my time knee deep in sheep shit? How will I find the strength to leave him for university after he's depended on me for so long? Why does it feel like choosing between my family and my dream?

Sliding my phone out from under the table, I refresh my emails, anxiously waiting for one in particular to appear. Still nothing. I suppose fashion school won't be an issue if I don't actually get accepted onto my course.

Grandad pauses for a moment, his eyes glassy, his frame looking even more diminished than it did only moments ago. He harrumphs. 'None of you get to drive Betty, okay?'

'I ain't fighting you on that one.' Jacob chuckles lowly and Grandad rolls his eyes.

'Alright Pip, crack out the chocolate biccies on the top shelf. These boys need to get their strength up before I put them to work.' Mum sighs in relief, a smile crossing her face as she does exactly as she's told.

CHAPTER 8

Seven years ago

'Kitty? You're home!' Those were Jacob's first words when I saw him for a surprise visit in the autumn. The first thing I did when our car pulled into the driveway was climb up the branch to the treehouse.

The leaves of the willow formed a carpet around the roots and a few strays were strewn across the floor of the treehouse. They were yellowed and dry and they crunched with each of my steps towards Jacob. There was an October chill in the air, but he was the only thing that stayed the same no matter the season. He hadn't even dug out his long trousers yet – his knees were still braving the elements, and he didn't look the slightest bit cold in his t-shirt. The sun hung low on the horizon this time of year, casting the trees and livestock in shadow as they grazed on the last of the harvest, fattening up for winter.

'Mum and Dad thought we needed to get away from London for a bit, Dad finally got some time off work, so we've come back for half-term,' I said, settling in beside him as he slid away his favourite atlas.

'You're here all week?' he asked with wide eyes. I nodded,

grinning. 'I have so much to show you!'

Without wasting another minute, he leaped down from the treehouse, not bothering to climb down carefully like everyone else. No matter how much of a rush he was in, however, he always made sure to stop to give me a hand down the steepest part of the branch.

'How's Hope?' I asked. We'd been raising that barn cat for a couple of years and watched her grow from tiny kitten to a fully-fledged adult that could catch birds bigger than her. I knew Jacob took good care of her when I was back in London.

'Proper chubby now. She eats more of my dinner than I do.' He shook his head, taking a slight detour to the Hope Farm kitchen for him to scoop up the camera that he'd got for his eleventh birthday, 'We can go and see her after I've shown you this.'

I followed him blindly into the small grove just to the east of Hope Farm. Hopping over streams and fallen branches, it almost felt like night with the trees so dense. Even without their leaves, the sun couldn't quite reach us, though the cloudy day might have helped with that too. Jacob pressed a finger to his lips to shush me, but I was too excited. I couldn't stop myself from breathing heavily, and the crisp leaves under our feet didn't help our sneaking either.

'Just through there,' he mouthed, pointing to the base of

an old oak that was all gnarled and twisted with age. I mean, it was a lovely tree, but unless it could speak or grant wishes, I couldn't see why he would have brought me here. I looked to him with furrowed brows, but he just pointed to the tree again without a word.

After a few more moments of silence, some of the fallen leaves began to twitch, and from a hole in the ground, a little black and white nose emerged. I gasped, but before I could scare it away, Jacob pressed a hand to my mouth, silencing me with an amused glint in his eyes.

We watched on as the badger sniffed through the blanket of leaves that had fallen around its set, nudging them around with its nose as though sweeping the porch. Jacob finally drew his hand away from my face as we both settled onto the ground. We laid on our bellies as we observed the creature from a distance. Minutes passed as we watched it go about its business, before the leaves twitched again. This time, three more badgers emerged from the set.

'Oh my gosh.' I couldn't help but breathe, and thankfully the family didn't seem to notice. Jacob did, however, and he smiled to himself.

'I've been watching them for a couple of weeks,' he whispered so quietly that I had to shuffle even closer to him to hear. One side of my body was pressed against his, and the autumn breeze didn't feel so icy after that.

'Did you know?' he asked. 'Badgers can eat up to two hundred worms every night.'

'Gross,' I said, shivering at the thought of anything eating those faceless things.

'Are you cold? Come here.' He threw an arm over my back and dragged me even further into him.

'Thanks.' I couldn't look at him to thank him, nor could I tell him that I was only shivering from disgust. But I was too comfortable and the idea of him moving away would be tragic.

Looking back now, I know that was my crush beginning to bloom, but eleven-year-old Ava didn't have a clue. I'd always felt warm and at home next to Jacob; I had just assumed that everyone felt the same way in his presence. But it was coming to a point that even my toes began to tingle at the slightest contact with him. I remember the way it felt for him to call me Kitty, to single me out from the rest. That's the memory that would keep me going right through until the next summer, fizzling with anticipation, and longing to be back with him again.

'The two smaller ones are their babies,' he continued and I had to try my hardest to concentrate on his words. 'They would have been born at the start of the year, but they're blind when they're born so they don't come out of the set for a few months. They're almost mature now, so sometimes they'll leave and start their own families, but often they stay together. They like the company.'

I could listen to him talk for hours. Sometimes, I did just sit and let him talk, especially when he had so much to say about whatever obscure new animal he'd learned about. It was funny – when we were around the others, he barely had one word to say. Sian told Granny that he's shy, and Will said he's mardy. But I'd realised that Jacob only spoke to people that actually wanted to hear him. Will, Lizzie, Alfie and Callum didn't really care to listen. They just wanted to be running around, or fighting.

'I bet you're top of your class at school, aren't you?' I asked. 'You're the cleverest boy I know.' I hadn't been watching the badgers for a while. I liked to see how his face changed as he talked about the animals. It's like he was reading straight out of an encyclopaedia in his head. I noticed he had a new scar above his eyebrow.

At the mention of school, however, his expression shifted and he sat up, holding his knees to his chest. He looked down to the forest floor. 'My teacher doesn't like me much.'

I sat up so quickly, the rustling sent the family racing back into their set. I grimaced at the thought of disturbing them, but turned back to what had concerned me first. 'What do you mean? How can anyone not like you, Wolfie?'

'I get in trouble a lot,' he muttered, picking up a fallen leaf and tearing it into tiny pieces.

'What kind of trouble?' The Jacob I knew was never told off, apart from when he walked through the house with his muddy wellies on.

He shrugged. 'I have to stay behind most lunchtimes to finish my work, and then I just get in more trouble in the afternoon.' A little anger flashed across his face. 'I don't get it. I hate it. I just sit in the same chair all day and I feel like my head is going to explode. I just can't pay attention. I want to be outside; I want to run around. The classroom is so stuffy! It feels like the room gets smaller and smaller every time I go back. It's like I'm trapped in there.'

Picking up a stray conker, he threw it back at the horse chestnut tree it came from. It bounced off the trunk with such force we had to dodge it on its way back towards us. I didn't know what to say, but my silence didn't deter him, so he continued.

'I don't get why I have to do all of that stuff. Those badgers don't go to school. They roam this bit of woodland for as long as they like. Just like the foxes, or the muntjacs, or the mice. And they're happy, aren't they? I wish I actually was a wolf, Kitty. They can go wherever they like and they don't get told off for tapping their pencil on the desk.'

'Maybe one day we can run away and live in the woods too,' I said, thrusting my hand into the pile of leaves.

'You'd come with me?' He looked at me, the pleading look of a dog in his eyes.

'Of course I would, Wolfie. I'd follow you into sets, dens, hives, anywhere you took me. I'd be happy as long as it was you and me.'

He smiled without looking at me, then spun around to lie back on his belly and we waited side by side for the badgers once more.

When the autumn breeze began to make the fallen leaves tremble around us, I tried my best to mask my shivers, but nothing could ever get past Jacob. Getting to his feet, he dusted off his shorts and offered me a hand up before I could protest.

We walked together in silence back through the woods. I wasn't sure whether Jacob was deep in thought like I was, or whether he just didn't want to disturb the other creatures as they began to stir in the evening air, but it was comfortable.

'Do you want to come with me to do my jobs?' Jacob turned to me once we had cleared the treeline.

'Your jobs?' I replied, and he nodded, with a little excitement.

'Mum and Dad think that now I've started secondary, that I should have some responsibilities on the farm. They put me in charge of sweeping the barn, checking on the chickens, feeding the pony, things like that. They're not big jobs, but it makes me feel like I'm actually useful somewhere.' He shrugged. 'Plus, Hope will probably be in the barn this time of night too . . .' he added, as though I needed tempting.

'Yeah, sure, I'll come with you.' He clenched his fists in excitement, then tried to pass it off as a stretch, but the gesture was already enough to make me a little giddy.

We reached the barn in no time. Jacob could hardly keep up as I moved even faster at the promise of seeing Hope again. And there she was, pacing the concrete as if she had been waiting for us to arrive, like my mother paced the kitchen if I was late home for dinner. As soon as we stepped past her threshold, she weaved in an out of my legs, pressing her face against my trousers with a loud rumbling purr.

'Will tried to pick her up the other day and she took a swipe at him,' Jacob said as she hopped happily into my arms to continue her fussing. This time, she pressed herself against my cheek. 'He was so mad; pretty sure she drew blood.'

'You'd never do such a thing would you.' I pressed myself into her fur, knowing full well she could take down a full-grown man if she so desired.

Whilst I busied myself catching up with my furry friend, Jacob got to work sweeping the barn until he broke out into a sweat. Setting Hope back down on her bed, I found another brush and set to work beside him.

'You don't have to do that, Kitty.' He shook his head, a

smile playing on his lips.

'Of course, I do. We're a team.' And with two of us on the task, it was soon spotless and we fell against a bale of hay, both out of breath and panting.

'You're coming to the Halloween party, right? Since you're here.' Jacob always had a funny way of asking – as if he was trying to be casual, slipping it in to conversation, as though he wasn't too bothered about the answer. But I always knew he was.

'Halloween party?' I asked, genuinely unaware of any such event.

'Has no one told you?' His eyes lit up. 'Halloween at Hope Farm is the best thing in the world. It's mum's favourite holiday and she goes all out. Costumes, buffet, party games, everything. Well, Will thinks he's too cool for a costume, but we all wear one, even Dad.'

'What costume are you wearing?'

He shrugs, 'I have a couple to choose from but they're mostly all of Will's old superhero costumes. I wanted to be a wolf, but we don't have any like that.'

'Well, if Mum does let me come, I don't have a costume either,' I said with a sad hum, and a small silence settled between us before the idea hit me, 'Why don't we make our own?'

'We could do that?' his face lit up once more.

'Yes! My granny has a sewing machine. I'm sure if I asked her, she'd show me how to use it. She taught me to sew by hand a few summers ago, but that takes me ages. It's really fun though, making your own clothes. Granny makes most of mine.' I had been trying my hand at sewing back in London, mostly just patching the holes in my trousers that I'd made in the summer. Holes in your trousers may be a common occurrence on a farm, but you do get a few funny looks on the London Underground.

'I can't wait.' Jacob grinned.

'Me too.'

CHAPTER 9

Now

The bus to college is supposed to be pulling up in the village in three hours, but already I sit on the edge of my bed with a sickness in my stomach. There's another message from Dad already on my phone:

Have a great first day!

I always loved school. But I loved *my* school, with *my* friends, doing subjects that I actually chose. Now I'm hundreds of miles away, and everything has changed. As much as I appreciate the voice notes Freya sends me to keep me updated with any gossip, it's not quite like the real thing.

I grip the duvet cover in my balled fists and it creases with the force and dampness of my hands. I can't do it. I can't walk into that college and pretend everything is okay. I can't walk out of this room and act like it's not killing me.

For an hour, I stare at the walls, sending myself crazy with panic. My heart pounds as my chest rises and falls until my vision is blurred from the tears.

Not knowing where else to turn, I take out my phone and

dial the number I've learned by heart.

'Hello?' Freya's tired voice flows through the speaker.

'Are you awake?' is the only reply I can think to give her and I picture her rolling her eyes on the other end.

'I am now. What can I do for you?' The sound of her voice now only reminds me how much I've missed her, how much I really need her.

'You could come and fetch me if you like,' I try and joke, but my laugh comes out like the depressed deflating of an old party balloon.

'That bad, huh?' She sighs. 'You know I would if I could, Ava, but I don't think the tube reaches that far. I'm sorry.' And I believe her. If she did have the means, she'd be here before lunch, but she's just as stuck as I am. 'What's happening?'

'I'm supposed to start college today . . .'

'Ah,' she says.

'How am I meant to just start again, Freya?'

'You aren't starting again. You do know that you still have all of the same friends, right? We're just a little bit further away. And in that place, you're not starting over. It's already full of happy memories,'

'And sad ones.' I interject.

'You'd be sad about those same memories whether you're in London or Timbuk-bloody-tu,' she chides. 'Ava, you've always got London, and you've always loved the farm. And you've got Callum – he's starting afresh too. And what about Jacob, won't he be in the same year? That's a good thing, surely?'

Hearing her say his name so directly makes me blink a few times before I can process her meaning.

'Everything has changed so much. I hardly recognise Jacob any more.' The thought of his cold shoulder makes me shudder. I tell her all about him not coming to dinner, and the tractor, and Pen, and she listens intently before tutting loudly on the other end.

'Why is it that boys go through puberty and all of a sudden, they stink? And yes, I mean literally and figuratively.' Her bluntness makes me chuckle, and some of the dread dissolves from me a little. 'Look, Ava, I'm not going to pretend everything is going to be perfect, and finishing your fashion A-level on your own is utterly insane. But if anyone can do it, it's you. I know how hard you work. I know how much it all means to you. All of this is just one more obstacle to tackle, and no matter how exhausting it all is, I know you'll get there. I know you'll smash it. Just stop thinking about everything around you for one second and remember who *you* are.'

'What if it's all for nothing and I don't even get in?' I think again of my empty inbox. My dream school has gone radio silent.

'Don't be stupid. Of course you'll get in. They'd be a fool not to accept you. And then you only have one year surrounded by various kinds of animal dung before you'll be living it up in Milan like the diva you were born to be.'

'The animal dung isn't so bad, you know. You get used to it quite quickly.' I chuckle, unable to find the emotion to address the serious parts of her speech.

'I'll take your word for it.'

Once our goodbyes turn into another conversation, and I spend another ten minutes on the phone, I am suitably inspired. Freya always knows what to say to make me feel better. When we finally hang up, I sit with her words for a moment, feeling each and every one.

With renewed strength, I get dressed, pull my portfolio from the wardrobe, and head straight out the back door for a little reminder of who I am. I find my way to the treehouse almost instinctively. I suppose, even when everything with Jacob feels so different, the treehouse is still the space I've always been safe. The knots and branches, no matter how much they age, have helped me get through so much, hidden me from so much, that it is the only place I can think to go when it all gets too much.

After tossing my portfolio into the hatch, I climb up behind it. Sweeping away a few fallen leaves with my hand, I make myself comfortable on the floor. Crossing my legs,

I open the files, using the surfaces of one of the boxes that was once a banquet table, or a treasure chest, or a flying car. Sliding through the pages of sketches, I find the one that is still unfinished and pull out my pencil case.

I had thought to call it 'the wolf in sheep's clothing'. From the outside, it's your regular suit: black, straight lines worn with a white shirt. But on the inside, its silk lining is bursting with colour, with vines twisting around the stitching, and lots of embroidery with leaves, trees and woodland creatures. It was meant to be all ornamental – the whole thing in such bright colours, is almost offending to the eyes.

'Looks good.' A voice startles me and sends my pencil in a rogue line across the page. I huff and scramble to erase it, but I only make it worse.

'Shit, sorry. I didn't mean to scare you.' Jacob grimaces as I look up at him. He's in a pair of jeans, a t-shirt and an old jacket with a sheep wool collar. There's a rucksack slung over his shoulder.

'How do you do that?' I ask him, looking back down at my page. To my own surprise, I don't sound irritated, just curious.

'What?'

'Move so silently. You're like some predator, sneaking around.' I feel him peering over at my sketches and I lean a little closer to the paper to shield it from his view.

'Practise?' he says. I'm still not looking at him, but I can tell he's shrugging. 'I watch a lot of animals in their habitats and don't like to disturb them.'

'So that's what I am right now? An animal in my natural habitat?' I look up at him with a smile.

'It looks that way to me.' He smiles, and a little glimmer of his old self flashes across his face. Maybe it's the light of the treehouse, or maybe it's being so far away from everyone else, but at least I know my Jacob is still in there, deep down.

My Jacob. Except he isn't mine, not any more. My smile drops.

'What are you doing here?' I say, turning away from him.

'Callum said you missed the bus. I thought you might need a lift.'

My heart thumps faster in my chest as I reach for my phone to check the time. 'I—I missed the bus?' I hadn't realised how late it's gotten.

'Yeah.' He raises an eyebrow, watching me as I silently curse.

'You know,' he says, sitting down beside me, 'college isn't too bad.'

Once upon a time, he was the only person I could tell all of my thoughts to. Before they'd even registered in my own mind, they'd be spoken aloud to him, and he'd listen until I was all finished and nothing felt so heavy any more. I think about this morning, when it took me so many words to try and explain to Freya what I thought was going wrong. But it's taken Jacob a couple of minutes of looking at me to figure out what's got me so frazzled. I wonder, briefly, if we could still be friends, if he can still see me so clearly.

But it's obvious that so many things have changed.

'You've had a personality transplant,' I say quietly.

'What?' He furrows his brows.

'You used to hate school,' I say, not wishing to repeat my original statement. It feels too familiar, like I'm not allowed to say those things about him any more.

'College is different. I can at least do some subjects I'm interested in.'

'Your college doesn't offer the one thing I'm interested in.' I can't help it; the misery overcomes me again. I grow a bit deflated. 'A whole year of work down the drain just for me to have to start again.'

'It doesn't look like it's gone down the drain to me.' Jacob rests a finger on the page of my portfolio, preventing me from closing it or hiding it away. 'You have real talent, Kitty. You won't need an A-level in fashion to prove you're good at what you do. Come on, just give college a chance. You never know . . . you might enjoy it.'

Jacob gets to his feet and stretches out his hand for me to take. I want to be stubborn. I want to stay angry. But the offer of his hand is too much to refuse. So, I take it, and follow him to my feet.

'One day,' I warn him. 'If you're lying and it sucks, I will never go again.'

'Okay, deal.' He smiles.

One of his front teeth is slightly chipped from when he slipped off the rope swing and fell headfirst into the bank of the stream when we were ten. He never cried, or worried. He got up, laughed, and swung right back across the stream to me, still bleeding, still smiling. I'm glad he hasn't had it fixed. All his imperfections are reminders of the Jacob I once knew, of who we both once were, and there's so much joy in each scar and crease.

The ride in Jacob's truck is relatively short, and we both say little, though I do text Callum a thanks, to which he sends a heart reaction in reply. Jacob taps the steering wheel to the radio, and my leg bounces erratically as I try my best to concentrate on the scene outside of the window as to not freak out completely. The greenery of the village soon turns to row upon row of buildings as the college comes into view. A litany of monochrome structures are surrounded by benches, each one occupied by students as they filter in and out. It looks like any other college – you could pick me up and dump me anywhere in the country and I'd be none the wiser from this clue alone, and something about that comforts me.

I can pretend just a moment longer that I haven't left London.

'So, what's your first class?' Jacob asks as we pull into the car park and he slots his truck into an empty space.

'Erm . . .' I rifle through my emails to look for my timetable. 'Photography.'

A smile stretches on his face once again. 'Well you're in good company. Let's go. We're already late.'

We hurry out of the car and he pulls me gently by the sleeve of my jumper. With no time to take it all in, I hurry behind him through corridor after corridor until we reach a door. From the outside, it looks just like all of the rest, but as soon as he pushes it open, I notice the whole space is filled floor to ceiling in photos, all of varying styles and colours, and I have no idea which one to focus on first.

'Nice of you to join us, Thorogood,' the teacher says before I can let my attention explore. 'And you must be Ava Matthews?' I nod without a word and follow Jacob to two spare seats closer to the front of the classroom.

'Sorry we're late,' Jacob apologises for the both of us, keeping his eyes low on the floor.

'Matthews, I'll let you off since it's your first day. But Thorogood, you can stay after class and help me reset the dark room.' Jacob nods wordlessly, as though he knew this was coming. I bite my tongue. I'm not brave enough to own up to the fact that he's late because of me.

Jacob taps his fingers on his desk in a structured rhythm that I know only too well. He taps the same at family dinners, or when meeting new people. He tapped just like that at Granny's funeral. He's anxious. I wonder if he'd have skipped his lessons completely had he not been trying to force me to come. Or is it the thought of his impending punishment, which is all my fault, that causes him to be so on edge?

Just like I did at Granny's funeral, I press the side of my own hand against his, and he freezes at the contact, ceasing his beat, and releasing a breath. He's a liar, I realise. He still can't stand school. But he's here because of me, I'm sure of it. Maybe he needed some bravery to come here too.

The rest of the class passes peacefully, though I have no idea of a single word the teacher has said. She spends the hour going through various camera settings and I have to lean over Jacob's shoulder to look at them in practise as my high-spec camera is just my phone. The tutor finishes her lecture with the promise of actually getting to use our cameras next lesson, and I can't say I actually hated it as much as I thought I would – but I'm not admitting that to anyone else.

'What do you have next?' he asks me at the end of class.

I check my email again. 'English. In the Ingram block? Whatever that is?'

'Do you know where you're going?' I shake my head, and

Jacob fusses a little, almost as if he's panicking for me before he starts giving me detailed directions. I nod, but clearly my face tells the actual truth. 'Hang on.' He pulls out his phone and taps away at it quickly.

'It's weird seeing you with a phone,' I comment. 'It's like seeing a donkey make a cup of tea. It's just not right.'

'I know, I don't use it much. It's mostly your grandad that calls me these days.' He shakes his head. 'I'd go completely off grid if I could, but I think Mum would kill me if she couldn't contact me at all hours of the day.' He smiles.

'Thank you for today, Wolfie.' I'm sincere, and the nickname feels like testing the waters for any sign of our previous life. My heart throbs almost painfully in my chest, but at least now I know that Wolfie is still in there, deep down. Maybe he is still the same boy who has hidden from the world in the woods with me whenever things get tough. Even though we're far from the foliage now, I still feel a little of what I did back then.

He doesn't seem to acknowledge what I've just said, though. Instead, he turns away to greet someone.

'Ah, here she is.' He grins towards the door as a tall girl strolls in, a leather jacket slung over her shoulders in a casually cool sort of way, making sure everyone knows she wouldn't be out of place on a motorbike. Pen leans into him, and he pulls her closer, kissing her softly. I'm suddenly very aware that I got dressed in a hurry this morning as a wave of nausea ripples through me.

'Hi Ava!' Pen says with her ever-stunning smile. Jacob's arm stays wrapped around her shoulder and they look the picture of a power couple. 'Jake told me you have English this morning too?' She takes my hand, genuine happiness ornamenting her features.

'Pen is in the same class,' Jacob explains. 'I thought she could help show you the way.'

'That's so kind of you,' I say to Pen, trying to hold back the stinging in my eyes and the burning in my belly. I knew they were together, I knew it very well, but seeing them stand here before me, looking so happy, so *perfect*, renews my jealousy once more. Perhaps I had just pictured them as good friends, just two people who hang out as a pair every now and again, but here they are, a fully fledged couple, embracing and smiling like fools.

'You okay?' Jacob asks, concerned. Only he has noticed the crack in my voice. Pen's face stays stuck in her beautiful, genuine smile, but it's making me feel sick.

I nod, burying my feelings. 'Just worrying that my Shakespeare isn't as good as it used to be.' I laugh, but it's uncomfortable. Jacob notices it too, because he still looks at me with a furrowed brow and an unconvinced expression.

'Don't you worry one bit.' Pen slides out of Jacob's hold

and hooks her arm through mine. 'I can get you up to speed. We can meet up back at Hope Farm. I can give you some of my notes if you'd like? And I'll introduce you to some of our classmates – I promise, it'll be fine!'

'You're too kind,' I say.

She kisses Jacob once more before we walk away together, arm in arm.

That's exactly the problem, I realise: she's too kind. Pen is perfect. In every possible way. You only need to meet her for five minutes to know. Maybe I could make myself feel better if I knew that Jacob had chosen someone that wasn't good enough for him, or his family hated her, or that she was awful and I'd be doing everyone a favour wanting him for myself. But she's not. Pen takes me to class, talks to me happily, and introduces me to our classmates just like she said she would. She even sends me all her notes on *Twelfth Night* along with a YouTube link she thinks I'll find funny. She is nothing but sweet and welcoming.

There is no wonder Jacob doesn't want me, when the woman he's with is created by the bloody heavens.

I hate college.

CHAPTER 10

Seven years ago

'One wolf costume, one kitten costume, and one red Power Ranger.' Granny stood up from her sewing machine, a little sweat beading on her upper lip as she handed each of us our costumes before collapsing into her armchair. 'Now, next time you decide you want outfits for you Halloween party, please give me a bit more notice than the night before.'

Granny was a wizard when it came to sewing. She could turn old bedsheets, old clothes, and scraps of fabric into the most amazing outfits or costumes. It's like her hands didn't hurt her when she was sliding materials through the machine, her ankles weren't so swollen as she pressed the pedals. Her fingers managed to wind up the bobbins with such speed and perfection, it's amazing to think she was the same woman that could only use one finger to type on a keyboard. That sewing machine wasn't just a sewing machine, I was sure of it. It was a time machine, and whenever she sat down at it, she was young again.

'Thank you, Granny.' I kissed her on the cheek and skipped out of the house with two of the costumes slung over my shoulder.

'Knock knock,' I said as I reached the treehouse. Jacob was already inside, his nose buried in a book. At the sound of my voice, he slammed it shut and offered me his full attention.

'You came!' Jacob clambered to his feet and grinned so wide that I could see he'd lost another tooth.

'I brought you a present.' My smile matched his as I drew the wolf costume from behind my back. 'I asked Granny to make you one like mine, so we can match. But mine is a cat, of course.'

'Mine's a wolf?' he asked with wide-eyed excitement. When I nodded, he pulled me into a tight hug 'This is the best thing in the world.' He held it up to admire it. 'Thank you, Kitty.'

'It was Granny that made it.' I laughed, trying my hardest to not let my cheeks turn too red. 'Well, she let me hand sew the ears, that's why they're a little bit wonky.'

'They're perfect.' He grinned, and raced to put them on his head, 'I think you should come to our Halloween party every year, and every year from now we will match.'

'Deal.' I smiled, fiddling with the bottom of my costume.

Once Jacob was dressed, we climbed down from the treehouse and made our way to the farm, both of us with an extra spring in our steps as I prowled on my hands and feet, and Jacob, as soon as the night began to fall, howled at the glowing moon.

Just as Jacob told me, Will was the only one not in a costume when we reached the barn. He stood beside Dave Thorogood at the barbecue overseeing the turning of the sausages, and scolded Alfie every time he ran too close in his Dracula cape. Lizzie was covered head to toe in glow sticks that I assumed were left out for the whole party to enjoy, but she wandered around like a lighthouse with neon bangles the whole way up her arms.

'Look at you two, eh.' Jacob's mum pinched at his wolf ear and he brushed her off with a growl. She had her face painted like a skull and a fake axe wedged into the top of her head. 'Very scary. I hope you cool cats and dogs—'

'Wolves!' Jacob corrected her.

'Sorry, I hope you cool cats and wolves aren't too busy scaring the neighbours to do some apple bobbing? I've got a pin the wart on the witch for later, and mummies too.' Her face lit up at the mention of her party games.

'Mummies?' I said and Sian only grinned wider, as though she was hoping someone would ask her more.

'Yep, I've pinched some toilet rolls from the loo, and you have to work in pairs to wrap up your partner until they look like a mummy.' She held her hands out in front of her and let out a deep groan before snapping back into her broad smile and pinching me on the cheeks. 'Oops, looks like we've ran out of brains on the buffet.'

She scurried back off to the table to replenish it, and Jacob must have noticed my look of disgust, 'Don't worry, they're not real. It's just pink jelly. She's got some moulds to make them look like brains.'

'Thank god.' I breathed. 'Would you be my partner? For the games I mean.'

'I'll always be your partner, Kitty. Only if you're the one getting wrapped up though.'

Jacob and I lost all of the games. Will, despite saying they're all for babies, won the prize every single time and Alfie spent the rest of the evening sulking by the bonfire. That was until his older brother clearly felt a little guilty and challenged him to a rematch, that Alfie won without much of a struggle. Jacob didn't seem to mind losing though. He danced with me through the barn, a toffee apple picked from the orchard wedged between his jaws, as he skipped around howling at the moon. For that night, he really was a wolf. He was completely and utterly wild, and allowed to be. And of course, I followed on his tail, leaping over hay bales, and crawling between bags of grain until we found a pile spilled, and instead of sweeping it aside, Jacob pulled me down to lie beside him as we made snow angels in the kernels.

I knew then that Jacob was the most interesting person I had ever met. I could follow him in silence, just doing as he did, and find every moment thrilling. I think I admired him back then, and I wanted to be just like him. I'm not sure when my admiration blossomed into love. Perhaps it was love the whole time, but all I knew at eleven years old was that being close to Jacob Thorogood was where I was happiest.

CHAPTER 11

Now

New message

Subject Your application to study at Istituto Marangoni, The School of Fashion, Milano

Those are the words that grab my attention in the subject line of my emails. It's an email I've been refreshing my inbox for weeks waiting for. It's an email that's kept me up at night just thinking about. An email that I can't now bring myself to open.

What if I've been rejected? Milan and fashion were my only plans, the only thing I've ever been sure on. I have no back up plan, I have no alternative options. Yes, I've technically applied to several other unis, but what is the point if it's not Milan? A degree in Fashion Design from Nottingham Trent hardly has the same ring to it. And if I get rejected, it won't only be me I've let down – what about Granny? It's all because of her that I know how to sew, all because of her that I can express myself through fabric and garments, all because of her that I had any sort of confidence to chase my dreams. If I fall at the first hurdle, all of Granny's lessons would be all for nothing. I can't let that happen.

But what if I've been accepted? Three years in Milan . . . alone. Could I handle it? Could I leave Callum behind? Or Mum? Or Dad? Or Grandad? My adventures have only ever been fantasy, made up dreams of woodland escapades or transatlantic voyages. The truth is, all of those quests that Jacob and I filled our heads with for a decade were never real. We never ran off into the forest to live like wolves, or escaped any further than the edge of this village. Our adventures always ended before it got dark, and we were always home for tea. What if I'm not as brave as I thought I was?

I don't know how long I've been staring at the screen of my laptop, but my eyes grow tired from the strain, and I still can't will my finger to click on it. In times like these, it would be Granny I'd run to. She'd know what to say. At least, after I explained what an email was, she would. If I was scared, Granny always knew what to say. Like one half term when we came up and I forgot my nightlight at home. Granny stayed up with me, telling me stories of good monsters and kind ghosts, until I fell asleep. From that day on, I loved the dark.

The sound of footsteps outside of my bedroom door finally forces me to break eye contact with my computer screen. I can tell from the long, rushed strides that they're Mum's. She never does anything slowly. Everything she does, she's in a hurry, whether that's work or the laundry or even on her runs. She always goes so quickly that it's a wonder she hasn't run out of steam yet. Maybe being here will make her finally slow down and smell the flowers, as Granny used to say.

Tucking my laptop under my arm, I drag open the bedroom door and follow the direction of her footsteps. I don't want to do this alone. I need someone to tell me that no matter what, it will be okay, and I need my mum, now more than ever. She's in her own room at the end of the hall, the door left ajar, but as I lift my hand to knock, her voice floats through the open crack.

'I just want it sold. I'm not bothered about maximising the profit or anything like that, just get it on the market.' I hold my breath as I listen to her speak. When Mum's on the phone, it's usually work related and nothing that interests me, but for some reason, I can't pull myself away from this conversation. 'It's a family three-bed. I'm sure it won't take long to sell, right?'

My heart drops so far and so quickly that I'm surprised it's not in a puddle at my feet. This isn't some stupid finance contract or some work-related thing she's being forced to do. No, this is my childhood home. The place Callum and I first learned to walk, to talk, and everything else. That place is packed with eighteen years of memories, of messy breakfasts, and movie nights, of falling into bed after long days, and knowing that I'm safe within those walls. How can she talk about it like it's nothing?

I try and regulate myself, pacing up and down the hallway until my hands shake so hard that I barely have control when I shove open her door. 'So, that's it then?'

Mum looks up from her lap, wide-eyed before murmuring quickly into her receiver, 'Sorry, I'll call you back.' She tosses her phone onto the bed. It bounces off and clatters loudly to the floor. 'Why are you listening outside my door, Ava?'

'Why are you giving up on everything?' The tears are so thick in my eyes that I can't see her, but I hear her sigh loud and clear. 'Why does none of this matter to you?'

'Of course, it matters. And I'm certainly not giving up. I am trying my best, Ava, for you and your brother.'

'And moving us hundreds of miles away, and tearing our family apart is what's best for us, is it?' A tear slips over my waterline and Mum picks at the corners of her nails. 'Is that all our family means to you now? You just want all of our memories gone?'

'You've only heard half a conversation. This is why I've always told you that eavesdropping gets you hurt. I thought you were happy here? You always begged me to come back to the farm when you were younger.'

'Yeah, well, everything has changed, hasn't it? And you'd know whether I was happy or not if you actually asked my opinion on anything instead of just treating me like a kid and deciding my whole life for me.' My knees tremble under my weight but I still manage to dodge mum's arm as she walks towards me with it outstretched for an embrace.

'You're angry, I know that.' Her brave face is slipping. 'I'm sorry.'

'Did you ever even love Dad?'

She's silent for a second, only the sound of my stifled sobs fill the room. 'That's not fair, Ava.'

That's all I need to hear. Mum doesn't chase me as I flee down the stairs and make for the door.

'Ava?' Callum catches me as he sits over his homework on the kitchen table, but I ignore him too.

I can't face the treehouse, everyone knows that's where I go to disappear, and the thought of running into Jacob at this very moment only forces me to walk faster still towards the one place they'll never look: the orchard.

Though it's still only the afternoon, the sky is dark. The clouds are so thick and full that the sun doesn't have a single gap to peek through. The rain is coming, that's obvious, but even a hurricane can't compare to the storm inside me I can't escape.

CHAPTER 12

Four years ago

'Your mum lets you drive the tractor by yourself?' I asked in surprise.

Jacob shrugged as he opened the cab door and summoned me to join him.

'Dad's hurt his leg and Will's been driving since he was thirteen, so I've been given some training. Besides, everyone's busy, and I'm the only one left to pick the apples. There's not much to it, and we won't have to go on the road.'

I gave him a sceptical look. If he offered me a piggy back, I wouldn't say no, but seeing the same guy that always had grazed knees and elbows from falling off his bike now in charge of heavy machinery didn't fill me with much hope.

'I physically can't go fast in this heap of junk, so you'll be safe, I promise.'

Granny looked at me with a smile from the porch. 'At least it's not a motorbike eh.' She shook her head and returned to her peonies.

'Fine, but if you make me car sick, I take no responsibility for throwing up all over you.'

'Deal.' Jacob leaned out of the cab and offered me his

hand. Taking it, he pulled me up into the tractor with ease and I settled into the seat beside him, already knowing that I trusted him more than I could ever trust myself.

'How come you're back again so soon?' Jacob looked at me from the corner of his eye.

'Eyes on the road.' He did as he was told with a smirk, and I was suddenly very aware of how close the seats were. My whole right side was pressed against his left so tightly that I could feel the heat of his thigh pulsing against my own, and rendering my throat drier than the fields in drought. 'Mum and Dad just said about us going to help Granny and Grandad for the weekend. I don't really know.'

Visits to the farm had become more frequent in the past few months. When we were really young, it was mostly just holidays, but then it started to turn into the odd weekend here and there too. Mum had said it was because Granny and Grandad were getting older and they needed extra hands on the farm, but even back then I couldn't shake the feeling that it had something to do with my parents arguing in hushed voices in the kitchen when they thought we couldn't hear. I wasn't a kid any more, at least I thought so at fourteen. I knew that things weren't always perfect, but the good days were getting fewer and farther between and I had started to wonder if they were ever good to begin with.

'Do your mum and dad ever argue?' I asked.

Jacob braked a little harshly at my question and we both jolted forward with the motion.

'Sorry,' he muttered, cheeks reddening. 'Erm, a bit. You know, who's making tea, or who has to force Alfie to put his pants on in the morning, the normal stuff. Why, do yours?'

'Yeah, sometimes,' I confessed. 'Do you think your parents really love each other?'

'I mean, they're always snogging in the kitchen.' Jacob pulled a face. 'It should be illegal for old people to do that in front of anyone. But I'd say they love each other, yeah. I can't imagine them being apart from each other.'

I knew the answer before I asked the question. Sian and Dave Thorogood always reminded me of Granny and Grandad; they bickered like their lives depended on it, and yet you could tell in every look, every cup of tea made, every smile shared in between moments of chaos, that they were a team, that they were in love.

Many a time I questioned why I too couldn't have been raised on Hope Farm, surrounded by parents who actually enjoyed one another's company, or actually enjoyed *my* company. Granny and Grandad were in love; I only had to look at them to realise that my parents were never going to last. But no child wants to admit that. I still didn't want to admit that.

Jacob pulled up to the orchard without either of us asking

any other questions and I was glad when I could disembark and take a full breath of fresh air again.

For a while, we plucked the apples from the tree in relative silence, only stopping to show one another a peculiarly shaped fruit or to take a moment of respite. But I could tell from the way he chewed his lip and drummed his fingers against a few apples that he also had something on his mind.

'Are you alright, Wolfie?'

His face softened at the name, and I was glad he was yet to grow out of it or think me silly for still calling him that. He threw the apple down and stood up straight, as if waiting for a chance to speak.

'Erm, well. It's, well, it's just that . . .'

My heart pumped faster as I watched him stumble over his words. He'd never been nervous around me, why now? Yes, I might have started to wear a bra, and I had dyed a bleached strip in my hair, but I couldn't keep up with the constellation of spots that wouldn't disappear from my face and I was pretty sure I was growing a moustache too. He couldn't all of a sudden see me as a girl, and not just some other animal in his kingdom.

But what if he did? He'd changed too. His voice had dropped so every word vibrated through me with its depth, and his hair had started to wrap around his jaw and chin. We were both growing up, and I wondered if he saw me the way

I was starting to see him.

'Ava, can I ask you something?'

Something in his whole being made me hot, made me lose my breath, made my skin tingle at the slightest touch of him. Could this really be him, confessing he feels the same?

'Anything,' I breathed, hearing nothing but his voice and the whooshing of my own blood in my ears. What if he kissed me?

'Have you got to pick your options at school?'

Like a hot air balloon struck by a fighter jet, I deflated.

'It's just, you know,' he continued in a rush, 'school isn't my thing and now I have to decide what subjects I'm going to need for my future but I have no idea what my future even is.'

My chest tightened and my stomach tensed. It was clear from the way Jacob paced the orchard that this was something that had been plaguing him for a while. Him telling me was nothing out of the ordinary – I'd asked him a hundred times for his advice on friends, on homework – so why did it feel so wrong now? Why was I so disappointed that his worry was so mundane?

I think I knew then that I loved him more than just a friend from the next farm over. I had spent so long wondering what love was, observing everyone around me, and I knew then, at fourteen years old, that he was the Grandad to my Granny. I think I knew by the way I felt about him that love wasn't like Mum and Dad's relationship – between two people that weren't even friends. I knew that I was in love with Jacob Thorogood, and I wanted him to know he loved me too.

But I pushed down my feeling, and I tried to be the friend he needed. 'Erm, yeah. I think I'm going to pick something to do with textiles and art. I want to be a fashion designer when I'm older, making clothes like Granny. I haven't picked between History or Geography, and my music teacher told me I definitely wasn't allowed to take music, so I guess I'll do something arty instead. Callum had all his picked in year seven. He knew what he wanted to do and I was jealous for a while, but he's always been a history geek.' Jacob ran a hand over his face and I grasped his wrist before the force of his palm could do any damage. 'What do you enjoy, Jacob?'

'Dad keeps talking to me about the farm as if it's all just assumed that I'll end up taking it on when I'm older. But I don't know. I love the farm, I do, but do I want to be a farmer? I don't know.' His words took me by surprise. I had always thought Jacob lived and breathed the farm, every spare moment of his day was in some way spent in and around it, helping his dad, or finding his own jobs to do. Even as a teenager, he could've taken over the farm without skipping a beat.

'You're thinking too far ahead. What do you enjoy, right now? If not the farm, what else?'

'This. Hanging out with you. Not having to sit and write in an exercise book. I don't know.' A little of my hope rekindled and I clung to his words, more than he could've known.

'Well, I'm afraid there are no GCSEs in hanging out with me, as far as I'm aware. How about something with animals? I don't know, biology?'

'They wanted us to dissect a frog in year eight and I couldn't bring myself to do it. My biology teacher didn't give me good grades after I refused and left the classroom. I know I live on a farm, I'm not naïve about death, and I eat meat, but . . . I don't know, I just like being with the animals, not studying them from a textbook or looking at their dead bodies in detail.' He shivered.

'Fair enough. But what about something practical, something where it's not all just writing? PE? DT?'

He pondered for a moment. I couldn't work out if he was trying to come up with an excuse for both, or genuinely considering it, but his musing was interrupted.

'Wait, shhh.' Jacob pressed his hand to my mouth in a sudden change of character, and he gestured with his head towards the line of trees. I could only watch him, wide-eyed, enveloped by the sweet smell of apples mixed with tractor oil that stained his hand. 'Stay here.'

I was too stunned to move even if I wanted to, and my eyes tracked his slow movements back to the tractor. Jacob pulled something from the cab and crept back towards me. An old film camera rested in his hands. He pressed a few buttons, wound a wheel, and lifted the viewfinder to his eye. I followed the direction of his gaze, until I settled on a doe in the field beside us, scouting out her surroundings, and looking over the land like it belonged only to her. My grin was difficult to stifle as I watched the scene play out, my lips still tingling from his touch. He moved like an animal himself – he was sleek, careful and elegant as he stepped around foliage and baskets to achieve the best angle. The twitching in his fingers had shifted from an anxious tremor to a deft command over his camera. Completely absorbed, it was clear that there was in fact something else he enjoyed.

'I think we've found you a subject,' I whispered. He took a moment of respite from his lens to shoot me an award-winning smile, and all of a sudden I was jealous that I didn't have a camera in my own hands to capture this moment.

CHAPTER 13

Now

Relentless rain pummels down the orchard for what feels like an age. The leaves have already begun to fall and the gaps in the branches don't offer much in the way of shelter. So, I sit curled up at the root of the tree, crying into the raindrops. It doesn't take long for it to soak through my clothes, my hair, my bones, until a cold coat clings to me and forces me to tremble. Still, it's not enough to make me want to go home. Well, now that I have no home, it's not enough to make me go back to the farm and face Mum.

Jacob and I used to sit for hours in the summer rain, sometimes sheltered in the treehouse, feeling a rhythmic drip on our faces as it leaked through the holes in the roof. Or we'd be here, stealing the apples from the trees – they always tasted better when cold, crisp, and dripping from the elements. It was Jacob that found that out, of course. Sometimes we'd run across to another farm in the village and fill our t-shirts with their strawberries until they stained pink.

Lifting my head to the sky, I close my eyes and pretend I'm ten again, when my greatest worry was whether Granny was going to whip out the nail scrubbing brush at bedtime, or that the end of the summer would come too fast and it would be weeks before I saw Jacob again.

'You'll catch a cold.' A voice startles me out of my daydream. I don't open my eyes to see who it is. It is as though I have manifested him here, as though he heard my thoughts loud and clear from across the acreage and followed the call.

'You of all people know that's not true.' I feel him sit down beside me, but I don't turn to look.

'Can you remember that one summer – I think we must have been eleven or twelve – when it rained for almost all of August?' He is so close to me that I can feel the water drip from his hair and caress my shoulder.

'And we tried our best to stay inside, playing games, drawing and God knows what else . . . and that lasted for what, two days?' I'm scared if I open my eyes now, I'd be talking to a figment of my imagination, so I savour the rain on my cheeks and the warmth of his body beside mine.

'Spent the next three weeks piss wet, though, and didn't sneeze once.'

'Well, apart from when Alfie shoved that dandelion up your nose.' I laugh, taking a chance and opening one eye. I capture a glimpse of him, his dark hair soaked and almost touching his shoulders, the water puddling in his dimples as he smiles.

'Yeah,' he chuckles, 'apart from then.'

We sit for a while, both letting the memory linger, both feeling the unrelenting raindrops on our faces, not worried that we're soaked through.

'So, are you going to tell me why we're sat out in the rain like a pair of wet wellies?' Jacob asks.

I rest my head on my arms that I have wrapped around my knees and watch him with a sad smile. 'There's no "we" about it. You gate-crashed my party.'

'Looked more fun than what I was doing.' He shrugs. 'Want me to give you a lift home?'

Home. What is a home? Four walls and a roof? A space in a cardboard box next to someone you love? Or does it not really exist at all? My home was a person. Now he's unrecognisable. My home was a place where all of my family gathered to eat their dinner and talk about their days. Now someone else and their family will eat at that table while mine is spread across the country. My home was Granny's garden, and that doesn't bloom so pretty now she's gone.

Everything I used to call home has changed, and now I don't know where to turn.

'No, thank you,' I say, stubbornly. Despite spending God knows how long out here, I'm still not ready to face Mum. I wish I never had to go back. I wish I could just disappear and all thoughts of university emails and broken homes didn't matter any more. 'We never did run away into the woods.'

I blurt, remembering all of the times we each promised the other we would. After bad grades, or family arguments, or just on days where normal civilisation was too much.

'There's still time.' Jacob doesn't miss a beat. If this were even two years ago, he'd leave with me now, without another word, but these days, I can't bring myself to believe him.

'We can't. You have Pen, and I have university.' In all honesty, university isn't holding me back, not now anyway, but I needed to remind us both of the beautiful, model-shaped elephant in the orchard.

'You've been accepted to uni?' he asks, ignoring the mention of his girlfriend.

'I don't know. I have an email from them that I can't bring myself to open.' He looks at me like I've grown two heads. 'I'm not sure I'll be happy about either outcome,' I confess. Despite all of his changes, I still can't seem to hold my thoughts in my head around him. It's like looking at him switches off the filter between my brain and mouth and it all just tumbles out. 'Everything in my life is changing so quickly and I can't keep up. No decision feels like the right one at the minute. I'm so lost.'

'You won't know unless you look,' he says, as if it's the most obvious thing in the world. 'Plus, what's the worst that could happen? If you get in, you don't actually have to take the offer, and if you don't, one: you'll have escaped an institution that is quite clearly stupid, and two: you have the world at your feet. One rejection isn't the end of it all – there are more unis, more chances, so many more opportunities.'

Jacob grows more and more animated the more he goes on, as if it his own future he is trying to convince me of. I mull his words over in silence, but he takes that as more hesitation. 'Kitty, you'll be just fine wherever you end up. And the woods will always be there, any time you need to disappear.'

My heart thumps in my chest and the pressure on my ribcage makes it difficult to breathe. For the first time in weeks, I see a little glimmer of home in Jacob. It's not much, but it's enough in this moment where everything else feels so foreign.

The rain still persists as I pull my phone out of my pocket, finally with enough courage to open my emails. With one last look at Jacob's grin, I slide open the mail app. I'll always have a back-up plan: I'll always have Jacob. I'll be Kitty and he'll be Wolfie.

I refresh the app once, twice, then on the third I deflate. No service. I thrust the phone towards him and he rolls his eyes, though still smiling. 'Ah yes, the joys of living in the middle of nowhere.' He mutters, getting to his feet, and wiping his hands on his sopping jeans before offering one to me.

I take it without hesitation and he pulls me out of the boggy earth. We head for his truck. 'I'm filthy,' I say before climbing into the seat, 'and soaking.'

Jacob shrugs. 'I had one of the sheep in here last week. Escaped out at your grandad's farm and I had no other way of taking her back. I'm sure it will survive a five-minute journey with your wet arse.' I flush, but climb into the seat anyway.

As though he can read my mind, we head for Hope Farm. Neither of us says a word for the duration, either from suspense, or comfort, I can't quite figure out, but only the sound of the heater pumping out hot air on full blast floats between us, and I don't bother to hide my smile. A rainbow hangs in the distance, one village over, where the sun is beginning to re-emerge. Jacob notices it too.

Pulling into the driveway of his family home, he is the first out of the truck, before he runs around the other side to help me down too.

'What on earth happened to you two?' Sian Thorogood calls from the kitchen door as she ferries us in with a look of shock. 'I'm having flashbacks to when you two horrors were ten.' She covers her face with her hands and throws us each a tea towel.

'Sorry, Sian,' I say with a cringe, dripping onto her kitchen tiles. 'We got caught in the rain.'

'I can see that, duckie.' She shakes her head. 'Stay here, I'll get you some spare clothes.'

We both do as we're told, Jacob's leg tapping underneath

him as he waits. It isn't long until his mum returns with a stack of clothes.

'Now, as I am sadly only blessed with boys—' she gives the same pained expression that she always gave me when she'd beg to plait my hair before dinners at Hope Farm '—you're going to have to wear a couple of Jacob's bits, if that's okay?' I flush again and look to Jacob for permission. He doesn't look at me but nods, his neck turning red. It is very warm in this kitchen; the Aga must be on full whack.

Slipping off into the downstairs loo, I peel off my clothes and replace them with the t-shirt and jogging bottoms. They fit almost perfectly, except I have to roll up the legs of the bottoms so they don't drag on the floor. The smell of Jacob lingers in ever fibre, hay mixed with aftershave into a heady cloud of him, and I have to emerge from the small cubicle before it overpowers me completely.

Jacob waits for me outside, his fingers drumming on his now dry thigh, his eyes searching across my face for any sign of emotion. When he allows his eyes to wander, they scale my body up and down, as though he's only for the first time seeing his own clothes. I cough before plonking myself down at the dining table as if it is my own.

My phone has connected automatically to their wi-fi. The password hasn't changed in all of these years, and as silly as it is, there's something comforting in it.

Ignoring all of the messages finally pinging through from Mum, I go to my emails, refresh the page, and click on the email without wavering for a second.

Congratulations is all I need to read in the first line before the look on my face gives it away, and Jacob is at my side, my head pressed against his torso so tightly I can feel his heart hammering in his chest almost as quickly as my own.

When Sian sets down two mugs of tea on the table in front of us, Jacob releases me with such speed that it wouldn't be silly to assume that the embrace had sent an electric shock through him. Coughing awkwardly, he looks between me and a spot on the floor, his mind evidently racing over what has just passed between us. Is he thinking about Pen? Would she be annoyed to see us so friendly? So intimate?

Not wishing to fuel his guilt or mine any more, I get to my feet. Thanking Sian for the tea, I try and make my excuses: 'I should probably head home, Mum will be worried.'

Jacob nods, but doesn't meet my eye and all of the progress that today had brought in our friendship fizzles out on the kitchen tiles between us. We are back to this awkward in-between.

Waving one last time, I scurry out of the kitchen, 'Kitty?' His voice reaches me as I swing open the door. 'Congratulations.' He smiles, genuinely, before turning on his heel and hurrying out of the room.

CHAPTER 14

Three years ago

AvaMatthews_xo:

welcome to the 21st century…

JacobThorogood7:

I still prefer sending messages via pigeon.

AvaMatthews_xo:

Come on, it's not that bad Grandad!

AvaMatthews_xo:

Just think about it like leaving notes in the treehouse.

JacobThorogood7:

I just clicked on something on this computer and it flashed up with a shirtless photo of my brother.

AvaMatthews_xo:

oh…

AvaMatthews_xo:

which brother?

JacobThorogood7:
William.

AvaMatthews_xo:
Gross.

JacobThorogood7:
You're not the one scarred from having seen it.

AvaMatthews_xo:
I wonder who he's been sending that to.

JacobThorogood7:
I don't wanna know.

'Oscar's here,' Freya hissed at me from across the lunch table, a sly grin on her face.

Shoving my phone back into my pocket, I shushed her quickly as he neared the table, though my face was already flushed, and her warning did little but ruffle me. Swiping my tongue across my teeth, I checked for bits of left-over sandwich or prawn cocktail crisp before turning around to greet him with the most nonchalant smile I could muster.

Oscar Simons transferred to our school last term and ended up in our friendship group. Freya and Ash had been loved up since what felt like the beginning of time, and so, it seemed, had everyone else, so naturally she had made it her mission to make me and Oscar the hot new thing. We were quite literally the only two single people she knew.

But Oscar played the guitar, and he drew beautiful portraits in my art class, so I didn't resist her matchmaking as much as I probably should have.

'Hi.' He smiled, slinging his legs over the bench to sit beside me, Freya raised her eyebrows indiscreetly and I tried my best to not even look in her direction.

'You alright?' I focused so hard on my packed lunch that I was surprised it hadn't combusted right in front of me.

'How come you weren't around over the holidays?' Oscar asked me, a little disappointment etched in his voice that only made my blush deepen. 'I thought I'd get to see you at Michael's Halloween party?'

Freya answered for me. 'Ava spends most of the holidays on her Granny and Grandad's farm. What do you think of sheep, Oscar? Ava helps raise lambs in the spring.' I wished for nothing more than to bury my head into my rucksack until the bell went and we could all be saved from this awkward conversation.

'Oh cool, yeah, they're cool.' Oscar swept a hand through his long fringe.

'It's not just sheep,' I said, attempting to salvage the talking points. 'There's other animals too, but it's mostly an arable farm. We like to spend Halloween down there because my friends on the next farm over throw the best parties.'

'Really?' he replied, almost genuinely interested.

'Yeah, there's all your traditional stuff, like the apple bobbing, the costumes, the bonfire, but each year we all tell each other stories, sometimes scary, sometimes not. But because it is so rural, there's not even any streetlights, so you can't see further than the flames of the fire. So no matter what anyone is saying, it gets terrifying.'

'Don't tell him, but Michael's Halloween party was nowhere near as good as that sounds.' Oscar smiled broadly and it matched my own. Freya was fed up of hearing about the farms, so it felt good to have someone new to tell.

'Maybe she can take you one holiday, Oscar,' Freya butted in again.

'I'd like that,' he replied, and I nodded politely. What would Jacob think of Oscar? He was so pristine, his shirts were always neatly ironed, his hair was perfectly combed – so much so that he carried one in his rucksack to touch up the loose strands throughout the day. I couldn't imagine them having a conversation. Well, I could imagine Oscar trying, but Jacob . . . no, he was too unsociable. Any new faces and he was silent as a mouse and slipped off any chance he got.

'I was just wanting to ask you,' Oscar started with a slight cough to clear his throat. 'Mrs Dean has asked us to find a partner for the art show that's happening in spring next year. Now I know our art styles are different, but you're so good and I'd be an idiot not to ask the best artist in class to work with me. So, if you haven't already found someone? Would you . . . you know, like to pair up with me?'

I could feel Freya bubbling under the table. Her legs rattled the whole thing until it felt like we were on the set of Jurrasic Park and I quickly thrust my hand over her mouth before she could let out an animal-like squeal.

'I would love that. Thank you,' I replied calmly, while still side-eyeing my best friend to try and get her to control herself.

The next few weeks passed quickly, with almost all of my free time spent in the art room with Oscar. Sometimes, we could just sit together in silence, him drawing, me sewing or designing, but it was nice to have the company. When we weren't working together, we were out and about with the whole of friend group, him with the guys, me with the girls. We never had much to say to one another outside of the art room, but he often stole a glance at me across the pavement when we all walked together.

'Ava.' Oscar turned to me one afternoon as we fell a little behind the group. I looked up at him, urging him to continue. 'I was just wondering . . .' he trailed off, his cheeks reddening.

His silence ran slightly past comfortable.

'Yes . . . ?' I encouraged, very aware that we were losing sight of the group up ahead.

'Well, I've really enjoyed hanging out with you these past few weeks. I don't think I could have got through this whole art show project without you.' He coughed, but it was clear he had nothing in his throat to clear, except his nerves.

'Me too!' I smiled and he started to breathe again. 'We make a good team.'

'Well, I was just thinking if you'd like to keep hanging out, you know, like after the show is done?' A bead of sweat emerged from his hairline and he swept it away quickly.

'Of course.' He sighed in relief, and I continued, 'You're my friend, of course I'm not just going to ditch you just because I'm using your skills to get me an A+.'

Oscar's face twisted painfully. 'No, Ava, I mean—'

The sound of my phone pinging in my pocket startled us both, and without thinking, I hurried to get it out of my pocket to check if *he* had replied.

JacobThorogood7:

How long is it until you're home next?

The photo was of Hope attached, snuggled up in the passenger seat of his tractor, in my seat. I melted, there and then. Hope, home, Jacob – my heart couldn't take it all and for several seconds I stood there, staring at the message, wondering if this was his way of saying he missed me. I tingled at the fact he had messaged me first, the fact that he had thought of me, hundreds of miles away.

'Ava?' Oscar reminded me of his presence with a nudge.

I whipped my phone around to show him the picture, but his smile wasn't genuine. 'Jacob, my friend from home – from Granny and Grandad's, I mean – just sent this,' I rushed to explain. 'It's our cat, Hope.'

'Oh, that's nice.' His tone was deflated, and looking back now, after Freya had told me he had been planning to ask me out, this interaction keeps me up at night.

'Maybe I could invite him to come and see the art show? It's still a while until I get to go back again . . .' I started thinking out loud before hurrying to catch up with Freya to tell her of my plans.

I was so blinded, so wrapped up in Jacob, that I really had no idea.

CHAPTER 15

Now

'Miss Matthews?' The photography teacher catches me as I head out of class. Jacob lingers in the doorway for a second as I walk to her desk. 'I hear you have a conditional offer to study fashion, in Milan of all places.' I cast a long glance at Jacob, who all of a sudden takes a great interest in changing the settings on his camera.

'Yes, miss,' I reply, warmed that Jacob has been talking about me, even if it is to our photography teacher – who we've often found napping in the dark room.

'Congratulations.' She's sincere, but she digs around in the array of papers in her desk noisily, not looking at me as she speaks. 'Where is it . . .' she mutters to herself, collecting the huge pile of essays that are clearly in her way and dropping them onto the floor. 'Ah ha!'

She draws out a crumpled leaflet from the stack and places it on the edge of her desk for me to read.

Young Creatives Exhibition

A place for young people to display their talents to the community and industry professionals

'Now, as you're well aware, we don't have a fashion and textiles department at this college, so the exhibit is usually quite art and photography heavy. Don't get me wrong, there's some great stuff, but I thought you could mix it up a bit. Since you're late to my cohort, if you chose to do it, I could count some of your exhibit towards your final grade, and I'm sure it would go a long way with your university prep too.

'I also hear you're independently studying your fashion A-level? If you give me the contact of your tutor back in London, I'm sure we can come to some arrangement about this counting towards your coursework.'

Now it's my turn to not look at her while she speaks. My head is still swimming with the Times New Roman of the leaflet.

'Why me?' My furrowed brows give away my confusion, I'm sure.

'Mr Thorogood tells me on good authority that you would do our establishment proud, and I believe this could be a useful assignment for you, and your future, too.'

'I—I . . .' I trail off.

Jacob has been talking about me? Not only that, but he's been singing my praises? Why is it that he has been so awkward, so distant to me in person, and yet here he is . . . helping me with my A-levels?

Because he's my friend, that's what friends do, I remind myself.

'You take this.' Our teacher slides the leaflet closer, taking my silence as hesitation and not confusion. 'And just have the weekend to think about it, okay?' Nodding, I thank her before turning back to the door.

Clearly, the mention of his name has sent Jacob scarpering, and I have to hunt across campus to find him. Sadly, in the few weeks I have been here already, my directional skills have not improved, and I'm sure I pass the science block at least three times before I hear my name called.

Pen waves me over from a bench in the courtyard. She's sitting on top of the table, her legs resting beside Jacob who sits beneath her, scribbling away at a notepad in front of him. My heart sinks a little at the sight of them both together, but I smile at her anyway. Pen has done nothing wrong, aside from being too friendly, too beautiful. It's not her fault that I'm jealous of her, and the sight of her only makes me ashamed of my own feelings for her boyfriend.

'Please say you're going to do the exhibition?' she says as I arrive at the table. Clearly, it's not just to the photography teacher that Jacob has been talking about me. Except, this time, it doesn't feel so sweet. This time, it feels less like he's been singing my praises, and more like pity.

Do he and Pen lie awake in the same bed, discussing how

pathetic I am? I can't decide what's worse – their charity, or the idea of them sharing a bed.

'I'm not sure,' I say, plopping my bag onto the table and sitting opposite Jacob, who looks up from his notepad expectantly. The thrill of the last ten minutes deflates, as reality returns.

'Why not?' he asks, a little aggressively.

'I just don't know if I'll have time. I've got so much to catch up on in my classes, and Grandad needs more and more help on the farm.' I think about the hours we've been up in the last week alone, trying to prepare the farm for late autumn and the frost that is beginning to threaten each morning. All of that on top of all of the studying I do in between has rendered me utterly exhausted, and I suppress a yawn just thinking about it.

'Don't be silly, Ava. Jake says you're so good at your fashion stuff. You need to focus on what you want. I'm sure your grandad will have plenty of help on the farm.' She looks towards Jacob who nods into his pages. Riveting pillow talk, I'm sure: my fashion 'talents'.

'I suppose . . .' I trail off, trying to refocus my thoughts onto the actual issue at hand. 'My uni offer is only a conditional, and I do need some miracle to pass this fashion course without a teacher.'

Pen claps her hands together loudly and Jacob and I jump

in unison. 'Perfect. You'll do it. We'll come and have a look at the exhibition too, won't we, Jake?'

'Yes, can do,' he says quietly.

I could shake him. Why is he so different when we're alone? Why does he show hints of being the boy I knew, and now, he's closed off and guarded again, as though he hasn't just tried to help me get to uni without me even asking? Does he not want Pen to know exactly how close we are? Does he not want anyone to know that he feels at least something for me, even if that is just a nostalgic sense of friendship? It's like he's embarrassed to know me when we're around others.

'Thanks for helping me out,' I address him directly, hoping he will at least look me in the eye to reply.

'It's nothing. Miss Hill has been looking for more students to do that exhibit for ages. Maybe now she'll stop asking me.'

'Oh, right.' The high I felt is slowly seeping out of me like a tyre with a slow puncture. 'Well, I appreciate it.' I smile at Pen, who gives me a blinding one in return. 'I better head home. I'll see you guys around.'

I find Callum waiting at the bus stop when I round the corner. He has one of his earphones wedged firmly in his ear, whilst he chatters away with a boy I vaguely recognise from my English class. I notice a Warhammer pin hanging from the stranger's backpack, and that's enough for me to know exactly how they've managed to strike up a conversation.

They speak so intensely for a pair that must have known each other less than a week. They laugh at something with an easy, unguarded openness that has always seemed to come naturally to Callum and I've never known how he does it.

A little jealousy stirs in me. Even back home, in a city known for its coldness and its people's disinclination for conversation with strangers, he'd pick up friends on almost every street corner with complete ease, like he does with just about everything else. Most of my friends were Callum's first – he'd do all of the hard part, and then introduce me when I could slip into a friendship seamlessly.

When he spots me, he wraps up the conversation with a clap on the boy's shoulder and jogs across the road to meet me.

'You not getting a lift with Jacob?' he says, offering me his other earphone.

'I don't know what's going on with him at the minute.' I sigh, stuffing the earphone in.

'It's strange isn't it, coming back here when we aren't kids any more.' Callum looks to me with a comforting smile. 'Like, I don't mean we've aged since last time or anything. I mean, coming here was always for fun, always a place of childhood and adventure and excitement. Coming for the holidays meant it was somewhere special that we only associated with fun. It's weird coming now and having to live in reality.'

I had been trying to find the words for it, and as always, my twin has made the scrambled thoughts in my brain make sense. He always has a way of being the calm in the storm. He still feels it's battering winds just as painfully as me, but he's able to find the strength to steer the ship. He feels things, just like I do, and yet he always manages to see the light at the end of the tunnel – a skill I have yet to master. He grins as he speaks, as though this 'weirdness' is an adventure to him, when to me, it feels like the end of all I've ever known.

'Good first week?' he asks, noticing my sullen face and bumping me with his elbow.

'Define good.' I laugh dryly.

'You're still upright. That's something.' He smiles again, and I feel some of the tension I've been carrying since this morning begin, just slightly, to loosen.

'Are you doing okay?' I ask, weaving my arm through his to pull him close, like we always did when we were afraid of the dark or being scolded together. Sometimes, I think he downplays his emotions just to be able to be there for me. When Granny died, we just about went into hibernation together, curled up in my bedroom in silence, just trying to comfort the other with our presence. While I could have stayed there for an age, it was Callum that decided it was time to get up and face our irreparably changed world. I couldn't have done that without him.

'Oh, you know me. Always have a grand old time. Well, until they told me my history course is now on the Russian revolution, when I was doing the French back in London.' He shrugs. 'It's all just different, isn't it.' Guilt stirs in me. I have neglected my twin a little these past few weeks. I've been so concerned about my own feelings, and his smile is so constant, his joy so seemingly limitless, that I realise I haven't stopped to think he could be struggling too.

Quickly, his moment of hesitation resumes into another grin after a nonchalant shrug, as his nauseating optimism persists again. 'But it's only a year. Soon you'll be away in Milan, and I'll be wherever will have me in this country.' Perhaps it's some weird twin intuition, or I'm not hiding it as well as I thought, but he can see clearly that I am not coping as well as he is. He knows I need his positivity more than anything right now, and he'd happily brush aside his own feelings just to make me feel better. Callum has always been a better person than anyone I've met, and far better than me in every single way. I really don't know what I'd do without him.

'We've never been apart longer than a few weeks.' I had hardly given it a thought until now. All my life, I could always just assume that Callum would be by my side. I'd never be alone because my twin, my shadow, wouldn't be far behind. And now I'm just expected to live without him for three years?

'We don't need to think about that now,' he says, sensing my anguish. 'Besides, do you really think I will pass up on weekends in bloody Milan? Not a chance. I hope you get a room with enough space for a blow-up bed.'

Callum nudges me with his shoulder and I crack a real smile. 'What about me? Why can't I spend the weekend in Norwich, or Leeds, or wherever you will be?'

'Ava.' He looks at me with a look of full seriousness. 'It's *Milan*.'

'Touché.' We both laugh. The dimple on his left side matches mine on my right. Granny always said we looked the most like twins when we laughed. There was rarely a time we weren't laughing when we'd visit her and Grandad.

'Have you told Dad you got in?' Callum asks, and the weight returns to the conversation.

I shake my head. 'He keeps texting, but I can't bring myself to reply.' Dad never used to text. I'd be lucky to get a thumbs up emoji or one-word answers from him over the phone. He'd always wait to have a conversation until he got home from work. Now he can't.

'You should tell him. He'll be so proud.' My twin smiles sadly.

'He'll be too busy with the house sale.' I make the excuse and Callum sighs. 'And I'm too busy with this.' I hand him the flyer for the exhibition and he scans his eyes over it.

'It will help with my fashion and photography,' I explain. 'It could count towards my coursework apparently.'

He looks at me. 'You are doing it, right?'

'I don't know.' I pull my jacket tighter across my chest. 'I'm already so far behind in everything else. And I don't even have a teacher for the fashion coursework, just an email address that sets me work and marks things for me. It just feels like a lot of risk for something that might amount to nothing.'

'Or it might amount to something.' Callum shrugs, as though it really is that simple. 'You've never needed someone standing over you telling you to work hard. You've been making things since you were eleven years old with stolen bits of Granny's fabrics. You never needed any encouragement then.'

'I wasn't stealing them! She gave them to me.'

'She gave them to you because you'd already taken them and she didn't have the heart to tell you off.' He raises an eyebrow, and I open my mouth to argue before realising he is almost certainly right.

'The point is,' he continues, 'you've always known what you wanted to do. Like, always. I don't think you've ever not known. Do you have any idea how rare that is?'

I look at him. There is something almost wistful in the way he says it, underneath the cheerfulness.

'Don't you know?' I ask. 'What you want to do, I mean.' He's always seemed like he's got it all together, all thought out and perfect. He's never not been confident in himself, or at least, he's never shown any glimmers of doubt.

Callum exhales, and tilts his head back to look at the sky for a moment. 'No,' he admits. 'Not really. Like, I know I love history. I know I could talk about it for the rest of my life without getting bored. But now we're not in London, I'm starting to feel like my options are limited. In the city, it feels like you could do anything and you have the world at your feet. There's always so much going on and you're in amongst it. But I suppose living here has given me a little reality check. I'm on the outside looking in this time, and realising it's all much harder than it looks. What could I actually do, realistically, with a history degree if I can't be the next Lucy Worsley?' He pulls a face. 'Maybe I'll get into teaching. History, obviously. Secondary school, maybe.' He glances at me, a little self-conscious in a way Callum rarely is. 'I know it's not very glamorous.'

'I think it's brilliant,' I say, and I mean it. 'You'd be so good at it. You've been giving unsolicited lectures about the Habsburg Empire since you were eleven.'

He rolls his eyes. 'Hardy har har. You're just jealous you don't have my encyclopaedic knowledge.'

'But honestly, Cal. I don't think it's too out there to think you could be the next big historian on the telly, if that's really what you want to do. You've got to dream, got to give it a shot at least. You don't need to sell yourself short because it's hard, or because you don't have a posh name that does the talking for you. I'd watch your documentaries. Hell, I've listened to you ramble on about movies for eighteen years and know far more about *Star Wars* than I ever intended to, and couldn't shake this knowledge if I tried. You've got a gift, now all you need to do is take the leap of faith. If it doesn't work out, you won't have lost anything that you have right now. If you fall, I'll always catch you.'

'Cringe.' My brother replies with glassy eyes, forcing us both to pause in our seriousness for a moment to chuckle. He throws an arm over my shoulders in a rare embrace and squeezes me close. I know well enough that that is all the reply I'm getting, and that's all the reply I need.

We stand in comfortable silence for a moment, before he asks, 'You do want to go to Milan, right?'

'Yes.' It comes out without hesitation, and I realise that my advice to Callum is the same advice I needed too. I'm allowed to follow my dreams, even if failure awaits at the end. I want to make something of myself. So what if in three years' time I just end up back here, in the exact place I started? I'm sure I'll have learnt something. And if I don't? If I succeed? Well, who knows . . .

'Then I think you'd be stupid not to do the exhibition,' my brother says bluntly. 'You might even enjoy it.'

Perhaps I will do it after all. Having no time left in my day to think about Dad and the house, and everything else that's come with this divorce, sounds like a plan to me.

'I'd catch you too, Ava,' he says, without his usual teasing tone, and a lump forms in my throat.

Then, before I can reply, my brother looks at me with genuine pride. 'I love watching you at the sewing machine, you know. It reminds me of Granny, and it's like she's still here when I hear it rumbling away in the next room.'

I hold him tighter, and he places a hand over mine. We don't need words to know what the other is saying, we never have.

'You wanna walk into town and get some chips?' he asks. 'This bus is taking an age, and I dread to think what Mum and Grandad have cooked for tea tonight.'

I nod enthusiastically, grateful at the prospect of not having ham, egg, and chips for the sixth night in a row.

CHAPTER 16

Three years ago

'Not a chance you're going to wear that?' Alfie laughed as Jacob pulled on Granny's wolf costume for the fourth year in a row.

Jacob shrugged, and I took a swig of my lemonade to combat the dryness in my throat. He just about managed to shove his mop of hair behind his wolf ears, but the trousers hung like pantaloons around his thighs. I could have sworn they still fit last Halloween, but even in the few weeks since summer ended and the October half term began, he seemed to have doubled in size. Will used to be the tallest, but when Jacob's curls are at their most unruly, he pips him to the title.

I had to get Granny to add a little more room into my cat costume too. No matter how hard I tried to ignore the size of my chest, my t-shirts could no longer hide it, and the thought of drawing anyone's attention towards me was enough to make me feel sick.

The Hope Farm Halloween party looked vastly different that year. Will swigged from a can of cider, and since the boys had all invited some friends from school and college, we shifted from apple bobbing in the kitchen to disco lights and a smoke machine in the barn. Hope sat curled up on my knee, miserable at the thought of sharing her home with anyone, let alone with all of the noise that hadn't even reached its peak yet. Alfie was still tampering with the decorations and prepared his best chat up lines that summoned a gag from Lizzie every time he would say one out loud.

Sian had already been warned by Will to stay well away, but I could tell by the spread on the barn table that she couldn't help herself and just had to leave some snacks out, even if it was just to soak up some of the booze Will and his friends were drinking.

'Is she doing okay?' Jacob drew in beside me to scratch Hope on her head and she purred against me in pleasure.

'I think I might ask your mum if she can have a box in the kitchen just for tonight. She hasn't stopped shaking.' I almost wished that I too could stay in a box by the Hope Farm hearth that night. The thought of having to spend a whole evening around all the boys' friends from school, and having not a clue what to say to any of them, didn't bring me much excitement.

'That doesn't sound like a bad idea. Or . . . we bin off this party all together and just us three hide out in the treehouse until everyone's gone.'

I could kiss him.

'Jake!' Will called out before we could escape. 'The guys are here.' Jacob gave me an apologetic grimace and mouthed a 'sorry' before answering his brother's summons.

Deciding against waiting for an introduction, Hope and I snuck away before we could be spotted. After finding her a warm spot in the kitchen, I set her down and sat beside her for a moment.

'I can do this,' I said out loud to the scruffy ball of fur. 'They're friends with Jacob, how bad can they be?' Hope purred in her box. 'They are also friends with Will though, and one of him is enough.'

'Who are you talking to?' Lizzie startled me as she made her silent entrance into the room.

'No one.' I blushed, and she eyed me suspiciously.

'I don't know why you think talking to yourself is better than talking to your cat, but sure, let's go with it.' Her smile enveloped her eyes as she sat on the other side of Hope and ran a finger down her curled back.

'I just wondered . . .' she began, and I looked at her perplexed. 'Well . . . it's a bit silly, really . . .'

Lizzie was always so sure of herself, always said exactly what she was thinking. What could've possibly had her in such a muddle?

'You okay?' I asked.

She released a long breath at the sound of my voice.

'I'm constantly surrounded by boys.' Lizzie shook her head. 'Which is fine if you need someone to climb a tree with and then jump down from the highest branch without worrying about any injury, but there are just some things that I can't talk to them about.' She plucked non-existent pieces of hay from her costume. She'd decided to come as a Jedi this year, hooded cloak, lightsabre and all. It was a rather interesting step up from the previous year, when she came as an apple core. No idea how she pulled it off with just hand-made papier Mache but I think sometimes it's best not to ask.

'Well, I can't say I'll be much good to you either,' I said, 'but you know I'm always here to try, right?'

Lizzie reached over Hope's box to clasp me by the hands. 'Has Jacob told you about our Christmas prom?'

I shook my head.

'Well, it's nothing serious. It's just what they decide to call discos now, which is stupid because disco sounds far more exciting.'

'Lizzie, focus.' I couldn't help but chuckle at the way she danced around her point.

'But it's so pathetic and really not me, and I'm embarrassed for even being bothered.'

I flashed her a stern look.

'Fine . . . I don't know what to wear.' She mumbled it under her breath, but I caught it loud and clear.

I don't think I had seen her in anything but cut-off jeans and hand-me-down t-shirts from one of her cousins before, so I could understand her conflict. 'Well, what would you feel most comfortable in?'

'Are pyjamas an option?' She ran a hand down her face so roughly that she was beginning to have the look of Darth Maul about her.

'You know you don't have to pretend to be someone completely different to these things, right?' I asked gently.

'But I want to look nice. I'm constantly in scruffy clothes and I'm starting to think people at school think I'm one of the animals that live on the farm.' My heart ached for her. Lizzie, despite her bossiness when it came to playing pretend, was a girl crafted entirely of kindness. Not a bad bone grew in her body, she worked harder than any Thorogood boy, and loved her family more than anything in the world. The thought of anyone having any sort of negative opinion of her made my big-sister instincts kick in. I knew I had to do something.

'Why don't we make you something? Something that looks fancy, but is still you, and still comfy?'

'Make something?' She furrowed her brows.

'Yeah! I could take your measurements while I'm still here and borrow Granny's sewing machine. I'm sure she won't mind. She's been teaching me a few different stitches and things, so I reckon it will be good practise.' I had been looking for every excuse to find a fashion project. Both Callum and I were fed up of me making him various embroidered shirts – they weren't exactly the latest trend for a fifteen-year-old boy. I longed for someone to dress up, and Lizzie was the closest thing I had.

'You'd do that for me?'

'Of course. It'll be fun, *and* it will give me something to do when I don't have you guys to entertain me.' She sighed with relief this time and leaned over the box, planting the heaviest kiss on my forehead that I'd ever received.

'You're amazing.' She grinned. 'Thank you.'

'Have you got a date for the evening?' I wiggled my eyebrows and she rolled her eyes.

'Nope. I was hoping that if I look a little better put together then I can maybe pre-order a date for next year. But honestly, I'm not bothered. I'll know enough people there. I was hoping Jake or Alfie would keep me company, but apparently Pen is going to ask Jake, so I'll be stuck with Alfie, and you know how much anyone would love that.'

'Jacob has a date?' My ears pricked up at the sound of his name. Sweat began to prickle at the back of my neck and on my palms and I shifted away from the fireplace, hoping to get away from its heat.

'No, Pen in his year *wants* to ask him. I'm not sure he'll say yes though. He's too busy rolling around like a pig in the mud to notice girls.'

I hardly heard what she was saying, my ears rang as I tried to imagine Jacob at a 'prom' at all, let alone with a girl on his arm.

'The only girl I've ever seen him with that's not family is you. I can't imagine him on a date.' She faked a gag and I almost felt the real thing overcome me.

And Pen? *Who is Pen?* I thought. I had never heard him mention her before. Why wouldn't he have brought her up if they were close enough to go to a dance together? My mind raced a million miles a minute trying to picture this girl, picture her with Jacob, until my stomach twisted itself into knots and I was starting to regret the toffee apple I had snuck from the buffet earlier.

'What's she like?' I asked. I'm not sure I really wanted to know, but I couldn't stop myself.

'Pen? She's nice. She's musical and pretty. One of the popular girls at school, but she isn't a cow about it.' I was praying Lizzie would say the opposite. Not that I'd wish for Jacob to be with someone awful, but the twisting in my gut couldn't handle the thought of them being well-suited. 'You'll have to meet her. I think he invited her tonight.'

I tried to smile and nodded, trying not to let on that I now wished to walk in that party less now than ever.

'I'm not sure Jake will go with her though, he's so

preoccupied with pining after y—'

'You know you guys are missing the party, right?' Callum cut her off as he wandered into the kitchen, his Yoda costume already covered in the green paint from his face. At the sound of his voice, Lizzie froze, and without finishing her sentence, she threw both her legs over the sill of the ground floor window and hopped down into the dark of the night, as though fleeing from an intergalactic villain. Both Callum and I were left staring, open mouthed, too stunned to even move.

'She okay?' Callum finally spoke after a few beats of silence passed between us as we tried to figure out what we'd just seen.

'No idea. We were talking about her going to prom, and then you showed up and you must have scared her in your costume.' I looked him up and down. I'm pretty sure he'd fashioned a few old potato sacks into a cloak and rubbed his face against a tray of face paint. His lack of talent in costume making was scary, but other than that, it was pretty tame. He just looked like a sack of sprouts, if he hadn't been walking around muddling the syntax in all of his sentences. 'Did you match with Lizzie on purpose?' I asked my brother.

He ignored me. 'She's been asked to the prom?' Callum asked wide-eyed, focusing on the unimportant part of my sentence.

'You knew about this thing too?' I shook my head. Why

was I always the last to know?

'Alfie only just told me, because the girl Jake is going with just arrived.'

With a little fire in my belly, mixed with the painful discomfort of an emotion I couldn't explain and a desire to know who this 'Pen' was that everyone just couldn't stop talking about, I planted an aggressive kiss on Hope's head and dragged my brother back to the barn.

The music thumped through the yard as various teens hobbled in and out of the doors, already acting wasted despite the fact the party had only been on for an hour, and the only booze on offer was cider. I followed Callum, who navigated his way through the crowd of strangers with ease and brought us out at the back of the barn where Will, Jacob, and a few others gathered, alongside a girl I assumed was Pen. Alfie was no doubt swinging from the rafters, and I dreaded to think what he'd have broken by morning – bones and all.

Though I knew she was only our age, Pen seemed so much older – like I was stuck in girlhood, and she was a fully fledged woman. She didn't try and hide her chest under layers of four-year-old cat costume. No, she stood confidently with every one of her curves on display. I could never imagine her looking in a mirror and hating anything she saw. She had a nose piercing and stacks of rings and necklaces, and everything about her felt so proper, so confident, that I cowered in her presence.

'You must be Ava!' She grinned and waved from across the group. 'I've heard so much about you!'

'Ditto,' I returned, my smile not as convincing as hers. 'It's nice to meet you.'

'Wait, do you and Jake have matching costumes?' She suddenly looked between us, and Jacob refused to look up from his shoes.

'Sort of,' I responded. 'My gran made them both. I'm a cat, but Jake is a wolf. We've had the costumes for a few years now. It's just like a little inside joke we've had since we were kids. I always said he was like a wolf, and well after we found Hope, our cat, he thought that I was, well, like a cat too.' I felt like an idiot the more I spoke, but Pen just smiled and nodded. As Will's other friends chuckled amongst themselves, Jacob flushed. Was he ashamed? Of me? Of being Wolfie?

'How adorable.' Pen pinched at the ears of Jacob's costume.

People started explaining their costumes in various degrees. And when Jacob thought everyone had looked away to listen to another of Will's anecdotes, he slid the ears off his head and shoved them into his pocket.

I saw him, though.

Excusing myself from the group, I found myself at the drinks table. I was tempted to try one of the ciders, but picked up a can of Diet Coke instead and took a swig.

'Mind if I join you?' One of the boys from the group stood

beside me with a soft smile. He was redheaded, speckled with freckles and had beautifully set teeth that look like he'd only just had his braces off. He smiled wider when I nodded. 'I'm Adam.'

'Ava.' I stuck out my hand for him to shake. 'Nice to meet you.'

'A handshake? Very formal,' he teased, but before I could pull it away in shame, he took my hand in his and squeezed it gently, sending a shiver through me.

'You're one of Jacob's friends?' My voice trembled a little. For the first time in my life, I actually recognised that he was hitting on me. I had absolutely no preparation for this moment.

'Will's, actually,' he replied.

An older boy was actually showing some interest in me? I chanced a glance at Jacob, who was looking around the party with a soured expression. When I caught his gaze, he snapped away and returned his attention to Pen, who stood beside him chatting away without any sort of nerves or restraint.

'Would you like to dance?' I still don't know where my confidence came from. I was never a dancer. I certainly didn't feel like I could dance 'correctly' at a party full of teenage boys, *with* a teenage boy.

Before I could backtrack, Adam gave me a perplexed look that shifted into a grin and a shrug. 'Go on then. Why not?'

CHAPTER 17

Now

'It isn't stopping.' Grandad stands at the kitchen window for the seventh morning of the week, chastising the rain as though his shaking bony fist is enough to ward it off. 'The dykes are full and the back field is a bog.'

'It's alright dad,' Mum tries a comforting hand on his shoulder, but he paces too quickly for it to stick too long.

'It's not alright. It's too wet to harvest the tates, the animals need to be moved inside to be grain fed, and there's no chance I'm going to get time to drill the winter wheat.'

Farming is both a science and an art. It relies on so many variables coming together at the right time in only the correct ways, that it may as well be sorcery. Especially here, where rain is in abundance, and yet drought always seems to hit at the very worst moment. In a country where the weather is known for its inability to stay fine from one hour to the next, farming needs only the perfect conditions. How are you meant to plan around a weather system that can't decide on snow or sun in March, or cold or blistering heat in October? I don't know how grandad has kept going for as many years as he has, where each bad harvest has a knock-on effect, until his whole livelihood is at risk after one cold snap. It's a game of chance, a gamble that rarely pays out in full, and leaves you swearing at the sky in every season.

Yet, never once has the thought of quitting been said aloud.

'Can we help, Grandad?' I speak up, my stomach in knots at the sight of him so rattled, so anxious.

'Have you got a magic wand to stop this rain, eh?' he grumbles.

I shake my head slowly, and I see the guilt seep into his features at his rash response.

'Sorry, Duckie. No, you keep up your homework and then you'll never have to worry about all of this.'

'We can bring the cows in, and the pigs?' I offer.

Despite what he says, I'll always want to worry about this farm. Though Milan and fashion are my dreams, and I was born in London and lived there for eighteen years, I was raised on this farm. All the summers spent on tractors and chasing the rain are the fondest memories I have, and even if I do make it as a fashion designer, I'll always come back here to visit and get stuck into lambing, harvesting or any other task when they need me. And who knows, if my plan really does go tits up, then maybe this is where I'm meant to end up.

Granny loved this farm, and I loved Granny. Apart from sewing, the farm is one of the only ways I have left to feel close to her. By helping here, I can feel like I did back when she was at this very table, telling us about the changing seasons.

'It's mucky work, kid. Especially in this rain.' Grandad sighs and plops down at the table. Mum places a biscuit in his hand before he can even say another syllable.

'When have you ever seen me worried about a bit of muck?' I challenge.

He looks up from the table to smile. His wiry eyebrows have grown out of control as they hang over into his eyes. Granny must have trimmed them for him.

'Aye, we used to go through boxes of washing powder when you two came to stay.' He shakes his head at the memory. 'The kitchen tiles didn't stand a chance with you two running in and out in your wellies, or even in your bare feet. I cleaned up more after the two of you than I did my heifers.'

'And they always came home without a single stain,' Mum says.

Grandad finally lets Mum hold him by the shoulder, and he smiles.

'That was all your mam. I'm sure she enchanted that washing machine.' He places his hand over hers then looks between me and Callum. 'Go on then, kids. I'll ring up the 'good boys from next door though, and they can give you a hand if they're not busy. You'll need boards and bodies, and a good strong coat.'

With Grandad's permission, and the 'proper' farmers called, Callum and I find ourselves trudging through water logged fields to find the cows as far away as they can get, sheltering in the treeline of the woods. Will and Jacob are already there when we reach them, and at the sight of their help in the distance, they hop out of Jacob's truck to hand us both a flask of tea.

'Milk and two sugars,' Jacob says lowly to me as he hands me the flask. 'I couldn't remember what Cal likes, so he has the same, just in case I mixed them up in the truck.'

'Thank you.' I grin, warmed by both the tea and the sentiment. 'So, what's the plan?' I say louder so everyone can hear me. The rain has relented for a moment, but how long it will last, I'm unsure. All I know is I'd much rather shepherd some cows now, in this brief moment of respite, than when I can't see an inch in front of my face from the downpour, so I try my hardest to not let us get distracted from the task at hand.

'I can assure you, whatever plan you have, these girls will not oblige you.' Will chuckles to himself. 'Plan is, we get these ladies into their barn in whatever way we possibly can.'

All of Will's summers spent as King of the treehouse have put him in good stead for bossing around farmhands, it seems.

'Sir, yes, sir.' Callum salutes him, a silly grin slapped on his face. Will cracks a smile and shoves him by the shoulder.

'Come on.' He tries his best to be serious but, even under his layers of waterproofs, I see him smirk. 'Let's get this over with.'

'Just make sure you watch your toes.' Jacob says to both Callum and me as we all allow his older brother to think he's in charge.

The cows, with a little food encouragement, don't put up much of a fight. At least not when the dream team are employed. And they're as much ready for their heated winter home as the rest of us, so that probably helped. Just like old times, Jacob, Callum, and I flank the herd like mercenaries marching prisoners from battle, with Will pacing out in front, shouting out his orders. Though this time, his voice is deep, and it thunders through the fields and makes us all, even the cows, stand to attention.

Any time Callum manages to get one of the heifers to obey him – they're too afraid to walk beside him in his bright yellow rain coat – he lets out a loud 'yeehaw' and walks a few steps like a cowboy that's soiled himself, which makes Jacob chuckle every single time. All too familiar with the antics of my brother, I simply shake my head and try to actually finish the task at hand, just grateful that Alfie isn't here to encourage him even more.

Despite the boys' inability to be serious in each other's

company, only one cow strays from the group, and Jacob spends twenty minutes chasing it around the woods in just one welly – the other one briefly stuck in the boggy mud. After an hour, each of the cows makes it to the barn before the second onslaught of rain begins.

The pigs, however, put up a little more of a fight.

'Callum, Jake, go left, go left.' Will calls across the field like a drill sergeant, his arms flailing with every word, his sleeves dripping with mostly water, but a little too much mud to be comfortable. 'No, *left* you muppet!' he calls to Callum, who has done little to help and has instead spent most of the afternoon running around like he is the one being herded. Will's patience is wearing thin as the novelty of 'playing' with us again turns back into his adult seriousness. He sternly reminds us all of our responsibilities. 'Jacob, rear. Ava, right. Callum, left. *My* left.'

The laughter subsides and we are all forced to lock in.

By now, I'm ninety percent mud. It's in my hair, smeared across my face, and it seeps into my clothes until I'm sure I can feel it running down my legs. 'Ava, come on, catch her!' Will shouts at me this time as a pig slips past me and makes a break for it.

I've never been much of a runner. Freya and I usually spent our cross-country PE lessons hidden somewhere on the school field, listening to music through her headphones.

So, I'd say I'm rather ill-prepared for a wild pig chase. Despite what may be reality, I feel as though I run fast. The rain hitting my face stings with the force and I know I'm bright red from the cold.

But I still stand no chance against this pig as I try and hold onto my wellies, clenching my toes as each step in the mud feels like I'm being swallowed a little deeper into the earth. I picture myself as a child again, running through these very fields, pretending to chase fairies, or monsters, as the Thorogood's play the baddies, out to get me too. We'd run in circles for hours, our imaginations doing such heavy lifting that what seemed like a world filled with magical creatures to us must have looked mental to Granny, who used to watch us from the kitchen window.

But we are actually chasing creatures now: real, wet, slippery creatures. And though I'd say my efforts are great, Will doesn't seem to think so. Despite his voice being muffled by the freak weather, I can still hear him shouting his orders at me from afar. So, with the pig in diving distance, I stop dead in my tracks, watch it flee for a second, before turning back to Will who chases behind me, his face like thunder.

'Go get it yourself.' I fold my arms over my chest.

'What the hell, Ava?' Will doesn't have time to stop and take in my protest as he runs right past me, firing his middle finger over his shoulder.

Returning to Callum, Jacob and the rest of the team of pigs, I can finally try to catch some of my breath. Jacob grabs me by the shoulder and smiles. He doesn't have to say anything for me to know that he approves of my stand.

It was always Lizzie who would be the first to declare, 'I'm not playing any more,' when Will's bossiness would take over the game. Her juvenile pout would always do the trick in softening him up into letting someone else have a go on the swing, or with the biggest stick. Jacob and I never got involved. As soon as the bickering started, that was always our cue to slip away and do our own thing. Sometimes we'd watch them argue from afar, tossing acorns and little pebbles at them from the treeline, watching as they all blamed the other for the attack. We'd stifle our giggles then make a break for it as soon as their backs were turned.

'Come on, we'll leave him to that one,' Jacob says. 'Let's get the rest of them in.' I can't mask my laugh as I refuse to take my eyes off of Will, already in the next field, swearing at a pig that I'm sure is running rings around him on purpose.

Without Will here to boss us around, we manage to get the rest of the pigs inside without a hitch or a struggle. Once they're all penned in and fed, the three of us stand at the door of the barn, watching Will dive through the mud trying to tackle the same pig that hasn't yet given up.

'Should we help him?' Callum says, chewing on his lip, his

look of sympathy too deep to hide.

'In a minute,' Jacob replies. 'He's been far too uptight at the minute, thinking he owns the place. He needs a little humbling, especially if it's a pig teaching him a lesson.' So, we watch him, until our bodies cramp from laughing and tears streak through the mud on my face each time he opts for a rugby tackle and ends up face-first in the gloop of the field.

Even Jacob laughs out loud. Though the sounds he makes are muted and muffled by his hand, his shoulders bounce up and down and the sight of it makes me forget about my muddy coat, and my freezing bones for a moment. He's always hidden his laughter, as though each giggle is thieved, or each chuckle is forbidden. I've never understood why. He smiles broadly, chipped teeth on full display, when it's just us two, so I know he has nothing to hide, nor be ashamed of. Though, it does make me feel special, as though I am privy to a secret few have ever been shown, and seeing him smile in his fully unreserved form is a privilege that can't be explained to an outsider.

'Okay, okay,' I say between gasping breaths, 'he's been punished enough. Let's get him.' And with that, the three of us sprint from the barn like monochromatic mud-stained Powerpuff Girls and save Will from a lifetime of humiliation.

'Two hot chocolates for my apprentices.' Grandad delivers two mugs to Callum and me as we sit on two low stools by the fire. Despite having showered and draped ourselves in blankets, we both still shiver so aggressively that the stools tremble against the uneven tiles of the kitchen, but Grandad's look of pride is enough to make it all worthwhile.

'I should have told you about old Peg.' Grandad shakes his head. 'She's my oldest sow. I was meant to have sold her years ago. I only managed to get one piglet out of her in all these years. She has been good for nothing as far as farming goes, but I can't bring myself to sell her. You notice how her eyes look in two different directions?' He chuckles. 'I could just never bring myself to part with her . . . when she looks up, one eye at you, the other on the food bucket. She's a menace, like. Never once been well behaved, always the first to escape, and encourages the others too. But your Granny loved her, just her innocent little face.'

'You kid's did good.' Mum adds, passing us each a plate of food to try and warm us from the inside out a little faster. 'I was always useless on the farm – I'm glad I never passed that onto you two. Maybe we should have moved here a while ago.' She chuckles, but Callum and I share a look that only the two of us can discern, and neither of us reply.

'I'm going to head up to bed,' I say after finishing my tea in silence. Wearing my blanket like a cape, I float over to the stairs.

'Already?' Mum says, a shade of disappointment in her tone. Guilt rises in my stomach.

'Yeah, I've got some work to do, and I could use an early night,' I say, offering her a truce in the form of a smile that she returns. With a soft 'night', I make my noisy exit up the creaking staircase.

Sitting with my hot chocolate at my bedroom window for a while, I savour the day in my mind. With each meeting, Jacob seems more like himself. Perhaps he's finally forgetting about what passed between us two years ago. Or perhaps it doesn't trouble him so much these days. Maybe seeing me again has made him realise he doesn't have the same feelings as he did before. We've both changed, and maybe we've both changed enough that what once felt like love has settled back to the innocent friendship we've shared for a decade.

I can't say it has changed for me though. With each passing day that he feels more like himself, I'm just reminded of how much my body, my soul, has longed for him. My love for Jacob is threatening to be just as strong as ever. But having my best friend back, even in the small doses, feels like enough to help me get through Mum's thoughtless comments, or the reality of just how much everything else has changed. Perhaps I just have to be content with his friendship. After two years without him, I know that I'd rather have another chink appear in my heart every time I see him than be cursed to never see him at all. Maybe one day I'll get used to the pain.

In the distance of the darkness, a light flickers softly, like a curling flame just strong enough to catch my eye. The rain has passed over for the evening, and the night sky has cleared until the stars are visible and the waning moon lights up the fields with a silvery glow. Moving closer to the pane, I see the light is hardly visible, quivering in the window of the treehouse.

My breathing quickens until it casts a fog on the glass and I have to swipe it clear with my sleeve. Discarding the blanket on the floor, I no longer feel the cold as the thought of him, calling me there, after so long, after the last time, after everything, fills me with a feeling I haven't let myself feel for so long. It's Jacob. It has to be. It would never be Will in the treehouse, and Alfie isn't trusted with matches, so it has to be Jacob. In the place that's full of our memories.

From the sound of crockery clattering against the sink downstairs, it's evident that no one else has followed me to bed and they all still sit in the kitchen, guarding the back door. And it's not like I can all of a sudden decide I'm not tired and going to go on a walk alone in the pitch black without it looking weird. So, I have no other option than to sneak out.

Sliding up the window, I assess my obstacles. First is

the fact that my room is on the first floor. I can't jump; I'd easily break a leg. And I'm definitely too heavy to shimmy down the Victorian drainpipes that I'm sure are fastened to the house with nothing but a prayer. My only option, that doesn't immediately scream imminent death, has to be the horse-chestnut tree that has a stray branch reaching just below my windowsill. I've cursed that tree many times, when it's knocked against the panes in the middle of the night, or dropped its spiky conkers that I've traipsed on in my bare feet. But today, it is my saviour. Hopefully.

With a shaking breath, I pull myself up onto the ledge, twisting around until my legs hang out of the opening, and I stretch out my toes as far as they will go to land on a branch that can hopefully bear my weight. With a few heart-stopping moments, and very, very, tightly clenched buttocks, I finally manage to take my first step out onto the tree and quickly descend before I think too much about what I'm doing and realise that I'm not some nimble character in a fantasy novel with too much plot armour.

Finally, back on solid ground. I make a run for it through the garden. My feet snag on the debris left behind from all the storms of the week, but I don't care. The treehouse is soon in my sights, and the child-like excitement that flows through me is not like anything I've felt for so long.

'We haven't done this since we were kids, Wolfie,' I call

breathlessly as I make the short climb up. 'I was starting to think you'd forgotten—' I pull myself through the hatch, but the blood is thumping in my ears too loud to have heard the voices inside, my eagerness too childish, too thoughtless to have noticed the two shadows in the doorway.

So, when I reach the entrance of the treehouse, expecting to see Wolfie in his shorts with his encyclopaedia, and instead find 'Jake' cross-legged and facing Pen, both of them shrouded in the romance of candle-light, far too close to just be having a friendly chat, I freeze.

It's too late to leave without being spotted. They both look at me, open mouthed, wide-eyed, like I'm some wild animal clattering through their home and disturbing their peace. I'm sure my face wears my shock in a similar way, though the profound sadness that creeps in and stings at the corners of my eyes is something I can't imagine either of them are experiencing right now.

'I—I'm so sorry,' is all I can mutter, before I leap down from the full height of the tree, my foot smashing into something sharp enough to send me limping back to the farm as fast as I can, not stopping once to see if Jacob watches me go.

CHAPTER 18

Three years ago

'Granny?' I said quietly from the living room door. She sat by herself in her armchair, tapping her foot along to the radio as she crocheted.

She didn't hear me at first, so I observed her. She never knew the words to any of the songs, not even ones from when she was young, but that never stopped her from singing along in her own musical jibberish. She knew the words to all of the old rhymes and lullabies, though. She used to sit at the end of our beds and sing them to us quietly until we fell asleep.

The open fire crackled by her side, as she soaked in this moment of peace, where she must have believed the rest of the house was busying themselves elsewhere. Her hair was red once. She'd shown me photos, some of them black and white, others faded, but her hair was still bright in all of them. It was white when I watched her then. She always braided it over one shoulder when she went to bed, and I'd always felt that if you caught her plait in the right light, at the edge of the fire's flames, you could still see a glimmer of her old colour. I got my dad's hair – dark, thick, all the curls sitting in a heap that's impossible to control. I'd have liked to have looked like

Granny when she was young.

'Oh Christ, you frightened me.' She must have caught a glimpse of my reflection in the TV. Granny watched my mirror image through the screen, her hand pressed to her heart as though to try and steady it manually.

'Sorry,' I muttered guiltily, moving fully into the room.

'What you lingering for, eh?' She set down her crochet on her knee, and folded her hands in her lap, awaiting my story.

'Did you always know you loved Grandad? From the first time you met him, I mean?' I flicked the corner of my shirt back and forth across my palm until the tickle turned into an itch.

She pondered for a moment, only the hum of her radio filling the room, and I couldn't bring myself to meet her eye. 'You have boy troubles.'

I snapped my eyes to her wrinkled smirk and my cheeks flushed so dark I'm sure I blended in with her scarlet rug.

As I turned to leave, she grasped me by the wrist with her soft fingers. 'I hated your grandfather when we first met.'

Relaxing at her touch, I kneeled beside her, resting my chin on the arm of her chair. 'Really?'

'Yep. He was my best friend's big brother. He teased us *mercilessly*. Laughed at us when we would get all dressed up to go dancing, or roll his eyes when we'd giggle at the dinner table. I thought him the rudest boy in the world.' She scowled at the memory, though it couldn't cover up the ghostly smile on her lips. 'Then one day, I'm out at the dance hall, having a lovely time, and there's your grandfather.

'Now, let me tell you something. I don't think I'd ever seen him in anything but his wellies, anywhere but the farm. But there he was, dressed in his Sunday best, hair combed, face shaved, looking like a true gent. He'd come out with the only intention of asking me for a dance. He didn't dare ask me to go with him. You know what I said?'

'No?' I chuckled.

'Absolutely not. I left him right there at the bar and found someone else to dance with instead.' She raked her fingernails through my hair as she spoke. Had her story not been so interesting, I could've been tempted into a nap. 'He tried for weeks after that. Would go to that dance hall every Friday, stand by the bar, ask me to dance, then inevitably have to watch me dance with someone else. Looking back now, I was a bit of a cow, but I still hadn't forgiven him for pulling my hair when we were ten.

'Then, one week, he didn't come. I couldn't rest all night, thinking about where he could be. I went all the way back to the farm to look for him, and found him in the barn, teaching himself to dance, resting on the single thread of hope that I'd be nosy enough to find him. And that was that, I suppose.'

'And your friend?' I tilted my face to look at her. 'She

didn't mind that you married her brother? It didn't ruin your friendship?'

'She couldn't understand it at first. To her, her big brother was just some sweaty, hairy monster set on this earth to torment her. I was distraught. I'd fallen for Harry, but she'd always been my best friend, and I didn't want to lose her. But I think your grandfather spoke to her, just those two, and after that, she became my sister.'

'I wonder what Grandad could have said.'

'I've wondered the same thing too.' She hummed. 'But he's always refused to tell me, and sometimes, a little secret is good.'

With that, the sound of a tractor at the front window stirred us from our moment and the core of an apple hit the glass in summons.

'I think that's for you.' Granny raised a stern eyebrow. 'But you tell that Thorogood boy that he can come back here and clean my windows.'

Clambering to my feet with a smile, I planted a kiss on the crown of her head. 'Will do.'

'And Ava?' she called as I reached the door. 'I've seen the way that boy smiles at you. You don't have anything to worry about, love.'

Though I headed for the door, I had the urge to turn back and ask her what she meant. Did she mean Jacob? But Jacob hardly smiled, and if he did, it was probably at the sight of a dormouse, or a hare hopping across the fields. She couldn't mean that Jacob liked me? Not like how Grandad liked her, all of those years ago?

'You okay, Kitty?' Jacob asked as I opened the door. My face must have mirrored my inner turmoil, and I couldn't bring myself to look at him, to notice his smile.

Shaking myself out of my thoughts, I forced a grin as I finally met his gaze. 'Sorry, away with the fairies.' He had his hair pushed back from his face, as though he'd run his fingers through his fringe so many times that he'd trained it to stay in place.

'The best place to be,' he replied with complete seriousness. 'You fancy picking some apples?'

'Go on then.' I hopped up into the cab of the tractor and Jacob climbed in beside me. 'Oh, and by the way, Granny will probably kill you if you mucky her windows again.'

'Noted.' He blushed as he started the ignition and the tractor kicked into action.

'Is it just us?' I looked around the orchard when we drew to a stop.

'Is that okay?' He reddened again, his eyes searching my face for any expression. 'The rest of them are off drilling the east field, but this needed doing before we lose the fruit to the frost.'

'Of course, it's okay.' His sudden nervousness confused me, but I tried not to overthink it. 'I was just wondering whether or not to wear a hardhat if Alfie was going to be around on his usual apple-lobbing shenanigans.'

'You're safe from everything but gravity, don't worry.'

When we got to the orchard, Jacob jumped from the tractor and offered his hand to help me down. I took it, and his blush seemed to spread over to me as though I'd been infected with his nervousness.

The afternoon stretched on, with stolen glances, silly jokes, smiles hidden behind trunks, and touches fumbled over apples. Granny's words rang around my head and suddenly I was noticing every gesture, every curl of his lips. Each one filled me with hope that he felt the same. Soon the sky burst into colours so vivid it's as though the trailer of Braeburns had projected its hue across the horizon for miles and miles. The whole world became our orchard.

'I bet you don't get this in London,' Jacob commented, biting into his third apple of the day, its juice rolling down the shining skin, then down his stubbled chin where he swiped it away with his open palm. All I could imagine was the sweetness of his skin as the sugar glistened against it in the setting sun. As he swiped his tongue over his lips, I found myself mirroring him, the taste hitting me as though I was sampling the very nectar of Jacob lips.

'Sunsets?' I remarked sarcastically, hopping up into the trailer. Unable to hold the weight of my own body, I laid back against the spot with no apples and stared up into the wide sky.

'No . . . I'm not *that* much of a country bumpkin. I know you have sunsets.' Jacob slid in beside me as though it was the most natural thing in the world. 'I just mean one so wide, so uninterrupted, so free. No skyscrapers getting in the way, only clouds and sky so vast you have no idea where it ends.'

He was right. Lying there beside him felt like the edge of a new world. The sound of the natural world around us filled me until I became the birds, the trees, the breeze. I was the rise and fall of his chest, I was the goosebumps that covered his arms, I was the soft rhythmic beat of his heart.

I couldn't bring myself to say anything, but I didn't need to. I was tucked into the crook of his arm that had inched closer to wrap around me. My heart throbbed, and I could feel it pulse in every inch of my body. I could finally breathe again when he closed the gap and pulled me to him, and we melted into one another.

'I could stay here forever.' I breathed. The smell of him, mixed with the sweet aroma of the apples, enveloped me until I was sure I had landed in some sort of fantasy.

Tighter still he pressed me to him. We were so close now that I was sure he could feel my heart thumping against him, and I could feel his. I could no longer tell where I finished and he began, the both of us threaded together by the pulse of our hearts that beat out the same rhythm. I was in love with him. My mind knew it, my heart knew it, and now my body knew it exceedingly well.

Jacob hummed in agreement. 'If we can't stay forever, we should stay at least until the stars come out.' He turned towards me, his face so close, his eyes so dark that they reflect the sky like tiny planetariums.

'Mum would kill me if I stayed out after dark.' Reality began to hit as more of the light slipped away. But I couldn't move, even if I had wanted to. I was bound to him, my limbs only moving if it meant getting closer.

'Then we only have a few more minutes.' He slid his hand along my cheek, his fingers finding their way into the strands of my hair as he caressed me with such gentle affection that I shivered to his touch. Instinctively, I hooked my leg over his, my whole body urging to be as close to him as humanly possible, and then some. I could have transcended all of science in that moment if it meant him absorbing me into him and us becoming one.

'We should get back . . .' I whispered, afraid of what I wanted, thrilled by the prospect of what could be. He was so close now, that as I spoke, my lips caught on his in a ghostly caress, just enough to leave me wanting, needing more.

Jacob looked at me, and he smiled. That crooked, perfect, smile. He leaned towards me, his breath hitting my lips and sending them tingling in an explosion of feelings I'd never felt before. I need him. Desperately.

'Ava.' His whisper sent a tremble down my whole body as I jolted against him.

Thud.

My heart just about dropped out of my chest as an apple hit the trailer with an echoing bang. Jacob sat up with such force, that I too was pulled upright with the motion, my head spinning.

'What the—' Jacob started, but the sight of Will answered all the questions we might have had.

Will smirked as though he knew exactly what he'd interrupted 'Come on, lovebirds. Mummy says it's time for beddybyes.'

I could have punched him.

CHAPTER 19

Now

Callum finds me tucked away in Granny's old sitting room surrounded by various papers, all scrawled with designs I'd started and then crumpled in anger. Since I interrupted Jacob and Pen in the treehouse three days ago, I thought there would be no better time to throw myself into my exhibition prep. It has absolutely nothing to do with avoiding him; the fact I've managed to keep away from his presence entirely in that time is merely a coincidence. At least, that's what I tell myself.

'If you wanted to bury yourself, surely the garden and a shovel would be more effective than paper?' my brother says, shifting some of the sheets with his slipper before settling down into Granny's armchair.

'Har har,' I reply dryly, balling up another sheet and tossing it at him.

'Why are you in here? I thought you always worked better in the treehouse.'

That's where I'd do all of my homework. I never worked *better* out there per se, it was just a good excuse to tell Granny and Grandad so I could sneak off and hope to bump into

Jacob. Which is exactly the opposite of what I want to do now.

'It's too cold this time of year,' I lie. 'Plus, the wind would mess up my papers.'

'Ah yes, all of your perfectly organised notes.' He gives a pointed look at the pile beside me. The papers look like they have already been lifted and set back down by a tornado. 'Wouldn't want those getting out of order.'

I sigh and sprawl out on the carpet, not worrying about the fact my limbs push my drawings even further out of place.

Callum finally gets to the point of his presence. 'Mum wanted to know if you need a shower before tonight so she can put the hot water on.'

I frown at him in reply. 'Tonight?' I question. I was expecting to not move from this position for another six hours before I dragged myself to bed fully clothed. As I have done the last three nights.

'The party?' he replies with a tone that would imply that I am, in fact, an idiot. But when I still look perplexed, he continues. 'The Halloween Party? At Hope Farm? Come on, don't tell me you forgot. It's like the biggest night of the year.'

I had forgotten. I had instructed my brain to throw out any thoughts involving Jacob and that evidently meant that the Halloween party was taken out with the trash. So focused on trying to get a grip on the one thing I can sort of control in my life, I threw myself into fashion, and everything else has fallen by the wayside.

'Oh, yeah. I don't think I'll bother this year.'

Callum looks at me like I've grown an extra head and it's just told him to fuck off.

'Not bother?' he says, genuinely offended. 'Right, what's going on? You're being weird.'

'Nothing,' I say, in a pitch that's definitely higher than I intended. I regulate, then try again. 'I'm just not feeling up to it this year. I've got too much to do, and no costume.'

'Come on Ava, it's the one night you let your hair down. We can go and just be kids again. I'm sure Sian will have a sneaky apple bobbing station she's set up without the boys knowing. You know you want to see me thrash you as usual.'

My twin sure knows which buttons of mine to press and I narrow my eyes at him. 'As if. I'm *way* better than you.'

Callum chuckles, before turning deadly serious. 'It's on.'

Shaking my head, I stifle a smile. 'I don't know, it just all feels weird this year.'

'It's Halloween. The one night a year it's *supposed* to feel weird.' He nudges me with his food and I slap it away playfully. 'Come on! You know you'll enjoy it when you're there.'

'I'll think about it,' I say after a brief pause.

'Perfect. I'll need you to sew me into my costume at

6:30, please.' He hops up from the armchair and practically skips out of the room, knowing full well I'll be too nosey to miss out.

How is it that you can dread something at the same time as longing for it?

The Hope Farm Halloween party has always held a special place in my heart, but each year, change comes with it. From apple bobbing and toffee apples, to alcopops and strangers; I dread to think what this year will bring. And yet, there is a niggle of anticipation I feel when I imagine the smell of the bonfire smoke as the crisp autumn evening draws in shades of red and gold, and the sky is lit by stars and sparks aplenty. The urge to wrap my hands around a sparkler, watching it dance in front of me in a dazzling display is enough to leave me transfixed, at both eight and eighteen. My desire to breathe in that molten metallic aroma that only arises this time of year, is still as strong as ever.

Looking at my old costume laid out by Grandad in what must have been an act of muscle memory, I wonder if we're all too old for this now. Will anyone actually dress up? What are you supposed to wear to a Halloween party when you're too old and too self-conscious for children's costumes?

Jacob has probably thrown his costume out. Thinking of him makes my foot sting in a painful reminder of a few nights ago, and my foolish hope that he would be waiting for me. Littered with splinters from my quick getaway, I've been limping around the house all week, too afraid to tell anyone the truth. Mum has me booked in for an appointment with a physiotherapist for my apparent plantar fasciitis, whatever that means.

Each step is a reminder that he doesn't need me any more. A reminder that I am the worst friend in the world, thinking a guy with a girlfriend would look at me twice. I hated girls in stories that were like me – dumb, blind, and constantly forgetting the key rules of girl code. And yet, when he looks at me, I fall all over again, and all common sense I thought I had goes out of the window.

This time, I'm not going to be blind. Thankfully I have the physical proof of his ambivalence towards me, a constant reminder in the form of a sharp shooting pain that he is taken, and I won't be that girl.

'Christ.' Lizzie's voice startles me from the doorway. 'I've watched you stare at that costume for a solid five minutes without moving. Are you going to put it on or not?' She's dressed as Gollum, bald cap, false teeth and all. At least she never changes.

'How long have you been standing there?' I ask once I'm

over the initial shock of both her unexpected entrance and her interesting appearance.

She shrugs and takes out her teeth to take a bite of a strawberry lace. 'Long enough. I've been waiting for you, and you're not even bloody dressed.'

'You're lucky I have any clothes on at all with you sneaking around like a creep.'

She suddenly gets into character and skulks towards me in an unnerving squat, and I bat her hands away with a laugh.

'I was thinking of just going like this,' I say.

'What?' She looks at me like I'm the one that looks insane right now. 'Don't be stupid. Stick your costume on. It's tradition.'

'I don't want to look like an idiot,' I mumble.

I think if Lizzie rolled her eyes any harder, they'd fall out of her head.

She gestures to the length of her body with an exaggerated expression. 'It's a cat costume, Ava, hardly pushing the boat out or challenging all the societal norms of teenage girls.'

She's right, I'm being ridiculous. And if the person dressed like an overgrown naked baby with dental issues is telling you *you're* being weird, that should probably be your wake-up call.

So, I stick on the ears, the tail, and the whiskers and follow Gollum over to Hope Farm, still with a limp in my step.

Mum's already there with a glass of wine in her hand, helping

Sian and Dave with the spread of hot dogs, fried onions, and various other finger foods. She's found some devil horns from somewhere and swiped on her deepest red lipstick. I don't think I've ever seen her dressed up before. She was always too busy to come to these parties, too swamped with work to make an exception for something so seemingly pointless.

All I can picture is Dad, alone in our house, with nothing but his laptop for company, working into the small hours because he has nothing better to do. I wonder if he'd have liked these parties, or even Hope Farm. I can hardly remember the last time he came here to visit, aside from Granny's funeral of course.

Knowing that the only communication I've had with him are one-word texts, the guilt finally catches up with me. Taking out my phone, I pop him a quick *Happy Halloween* text with a photo of Lizzie and I in our costumes.

Brilliant.

Is Lizzie *Gollum?* Love it. Have the best time.

Miss you, kiddo.

Before I can get choked up at his replies, Sian spots us. At the sight of our costumes, she smiles so wide I'm surprised her fake fangs haven't popped out.

'Hi girls,' Sian says, as she prepares a plate of lychees that she's made to look like eyeballs, and pops them beside the little sausages that she's meticulously carved into lady's fingers. Sian Thorogood has always been the queen of Halloween, even in the years when her eldest son moaned at her for it being too babyish, or she had to hide out in the kitchen all night to avoid being spotted. Even when she knew she wouldn't be appreciated, she still refused to let the magic die. 'Make sure you grab a plate of food. There's plenty so no need to go hungry.'

'The boys are all out in the barn,' Dave says. 'But watch yourselves. I've let Will be in charge of the bonfire this year as a bribe to make him stay home and not go to some piss up somewhere in town, so just don't get too close.' Dave's regret is clear on his face, and the concern on Mum's and Sian's is also impossible to hide.

'Come on, let's go!' Lizzie slurs, the saliva collecting in her false teeth as she pulls me towards the door.

The smoke from the bonfire wafts in a thick stream across the yard and we cough and splutter with each step it takes to reach the barn. The place is already packed, some faces I recognise from college, others I don't. But there's one in particular that I can't help but search for.

He's not here. I knew deep down he wouldn't come. Why

would he? He hates crowds, always has, and Will's smoke signals are enough to drive anyone away. Jacob is more than likely off with Pen somewhere, snogging in his truck or—

'What's wrong with your foot?' His voice comes from over my shoulder and cuts straight through the cacophony of music and chatter, though it's almost a whisper.

Whipping around, Jacob stands before me, wolf ears, tail, and whiskers all intact, and a smile just for additional damage.

'You're here?' I breathe, trying to remind myself of the talk I gave myself only an hour ago.

'Why wouldn't I be?' He furrows his eyebrows, as though expecting a better reception.

'I thought you'd be off somewhere with Pen.' I can't stop myself from saying it and he sighs. 'I thought this wouldn't be your kind of thing any more.' I gesture to his costume, and he looks down at himself, confusion peppering his expression.

'The costume? You and your granny made this for me, and I've worn it for years. It's pretty much a tradition at this point. I wore it last year too, hoping you'd turn up last minute. Looked a bit of a fool on my own.'

All he does is mess with my head. One minute, he's the person I've always known, in the next, he's a stranger with a girlfriend and I can't keep letting my guard down. I can't keep falling like this.

Turning from him, I begin to walk away, but he grasps me

by the arm before I can put any distance between us. 'You still haven't told me what you've done to your foot.'

I can't stop the anger from bubbling through me. 'A mixture of thorns and splinters, if you must know.'

'From the treehouse? Why didn't you stop and let me help you?' Genuine concern presses on his features. 'I'm sure I have my old bug collecting kit still stashed there somewhere.'

'You were with your *girlfriend*, Jacob.' I shake myself from his grip and make for the barn doors, but he follows me.

Mum is tipsy in the yard, trying to catch smoke in her hands before turning to Sian and giggling into her witch's cape. Callum, dressed as Gandalf in a cloak I stitched for him hastily earlier, chats to some girl from college. Lizzie is nowhere to be seen, and Alfie seems to be in a conspiratorial huddle with some of his friends.

'What's that got to do with anything?' Jacob calls out behind me. 'You're in pain, I wanted to help you. We're friends, Ava, that's what friends do.'

'Yeah, well, I'm starting to think we're not even friends any more.'

His face transforms from anger to pain. 'We'll always be friends.' He draws in closer to me now and only I can hear his voice. 'Nothing will change that. Not London, not Pen, not Milan.'

I don't want to be friends. I don't want to sit at the side

lines and be forced to smile and congratulate him and Pen when they eventually marry. I don't want to have to pretend that I'm not overwhelmingly in love with him. I can't keep pretending.

But he's right. He's with Pen, who is practically Mary Poppins with an eyebrow piercing for god's sake. And in a few months, I will uproot my life once more to move across the channel. Jacob couldn't stand London, so it's not like he would get on a plane to see me in Milan. We've had so many chances at being something more, and none of them have ever worked. Maybe I've been clinging onto something that was never concrete to begin with. Trying to make a relationship with Jacob would be like trying to catch the copious amounts of smoke from this bloody bonfire that is choking me and sending my eyes streaming: futile, and I'd look stupid doing it. It's self-destructive.

Shoving down the pain that bubbles up through my whole body, I nod, and try and stretch a smile only my trembling face. 'Yeah, friends. We will always be friends.'

I turn from him before he can see me cry, and this time, he doesn't follow me when I walk away.

Everything else has been a disaster since I got here, why not the famed Halloween party as well?

CHAPTER 20

Two and a half years ago

Jacob made it clear he hated London during his one and only visit over the years.

I usually tried to avoid King's Cross Station like the plague. It was always too loud, too busy, with too many people walking far too slowly past the platforms nine and ten, and then being drawn into the stupidly long tourist trap queue of Platform 9 ¾. Or they'd try and walk too quickly out of the barriers, and you'd always end up in a bottle neck of sweaty suits, all trying to make the stupid things read your ticket fast enough to let you through the dam.

But on that day, I found myself there willingly. I wasn't travelling, so the stress was immediately diminished, but I still bounced my leg impatiently as I sat on one of those big concrete slabs outside that some overpaid fella thought was a better option than a traditional bench. Callum had disappeared to some sandwich shop around the corner, and I was anticipating him coming back with something the size of his own head, only so he could complain the whole bus ride home that he was too full.

Each time another train arrived, a deluge of bodies flooded

out onto the station floor and I found myself scanning each and every face for his, despite knowing his train didn't get in for another ten minutes. Still, I watched, as all of the unknown faces passed by, on their own journeys to who knows where, wondering what their story was.

The spring sun seeped out from behind the clouds, the warmth of it hitting my face as I savoured it for just a moment. After months of winter clouds, this felt nice. Basking in the light, I tuned out the sound of the road, the flight path, the thousands of bodies, until I was sat in the garden at Granny and Grandad's at the start of the summer, with six whole weeks ahead of me where anything felt possible. There really was no feeling like it: the freedom, the anticipation, the knowledge that I was exactly where I wanted to be.

When I opened my eyes again, the clock tower showed 11:52 a.m. Bodies flowed through the gates, though this time, I knew they had travelled through the countryside I called home. I scanned over each person until the last one sauntered through. But his face wasn't amongst them. Did I miss him? Did he get on the wrong train? Did he change his mind and decide not to come after all?

Getting to my feet, I headed back into the station, scanning each and every crevice for any sign of him. That boy could navigate his way through any forest, or make it way back home in the dark with only moonlight to guide him; surely, he couldn't be lost. With my heart thumping in my ears, I paced the platform, gnawing on my fingernails as I went. I checked the time again. We had only an hour until the show. If he was delayed, he would miss it, and this would've all been for nothing.

'Ava!' Jacob called my name from the opposite side of the barrier, relief flooding his expression as he grappled with various tickets and papers in his hands.

For just a moment, I took in the image of him. It seemed that every time I saw him, there was something that had changed: a new dappling of stubble on his chin, or that he'd grown an inch or two, or that he hadn't cut his hair for a few months. But this was different. He was almost exactly the same as when I saw him the previous autumn, and yet, everything felt wrong. It was like seeing a polar bear in the zoo. You know that it's possible, that they can survive there in their drab enclosures, but that doesn't mean it feels right.

After explaining to him how to feed his ticket into the machine, seeing as he refused to bring his phone to do it the easy way, he was finally before me in all his glory wearing . . . full length trousers.

'How was your journey?' I asked, trying not to mention the new addition to his wardrobe.

'I was quite nice actually, getting to travel through parts of the country you can't otherwise get to. Plus, it's spring, so every other field is full of lambs. And you know me and my lambs.' He grinned. I was expecting a moan, about too many people in one tin can, or the time it took to get here, but he seemed genuinely happy.

'Well, welcome to London.' I gestured to the streets. 'It's so strange – you coming to my house, in my town, for a change. I can't wait to show my friends that you're actually real and I haven't just been making you up all these years.' I wanted to weave my arm through his and have us skip down the path, but I tapered my excitement and settled on squeezing his bicep with a smile.

Jacob flushed, then coughed. 'Where's Cal? Is he not coming too?'

I had almost forgotten about my twin and his rather long detour for food, but I wasn't worried. 'He's around here somewhere, but I'm afraid his stomach came before you.'

'Standard.' He chuckled and we rounded the corner and found Callum perched on a ledge, scoffing his sandwich as though someone was on their way to steal it from him.

'Jake!' He lit up at the sight of his friend, and smiled with his mouth stuffed with various meat and cheeses. 'Welcome to London, mate!' he finally added after he'd scarfed down his bite.

'Right, we need to get going,' I declared. 'I said I'd meet the guys in the café before the exhibition, and it's at least twenty minutes on the bus from here.' My initial excitement from seeing my guest was slowly being overtaken by anxious thoughts about the thing he actually came for.

Both the boys stood to attention and awaited their next order in silence as I directed us all to the bus stop. Jacob didn't speak for the duration of the journey – he stared out of the rain-stained windows, watching the city go by. It's not like we passed anywhere particularly exciting – no Buckingham Palace, no Big Ben, no Trafalgar Square. Just the city roads were enough to captivate him.

We pulled up to the venue with plenty of time to spare, and found Freya, her girlfriend Ash, Oscar, and a few others from the friend group sitting at the patio table and chairs outside the café next door.

'Oh my gosh, you must be Jacob.' Freya stood at the bus doors and began her onslaught of chatter the moment they opened, confusing the young mum and her pram that reached the door before us.

Jacob lifted his hand in an awkward wave as Freya marvelled at him like a rare creature she'd only heard about in books. She had heard me talk about Jacob relentlessly for years without a single meeting, so I wouldn't have been surprised if she doubted his existence entirely until now.

'I've heard so much about you!' Freya dragged him by his forearm to the table as Jacob shot me a pleading look from over his shoulder. Introducing him to all of my friends one by one, they each smiled and waved politely, but no one else seems quite as fascinated as Freya – no one but her had listened to me ramble on about him for so long.

When Callum and I reached the rest of the congregation, Oscar stood up from his seat and gestured for me to take it. Thanking him, I sat down, and he leaned against the back of the chair, making sure his forearm pressed lightly against my shoulder blades.

Oscar leaned close to talk, but spoke loudly enough for everyone to hear. 'Before we go and see it in the flesh, I just want to say that I'm so proud of you. Whatever grade we end up with will be because of your designs. You've definitely carried this team.'

My cheeks flushed as I tried to avoid the eyes of everyone at the table as they seemed to find this the most interesting topic of conversation. 'Don't be silly. It's been a joint effort.'

'Well, I wanted to get you a little gift anyway.' From under the table, he pulled out a small bouquet of flowers, the kind that had been dyed into rainbows. The petals were so heavy with artificial colour they could've wilted at any moment.

'You really shouldn't have.' Standing up to thank him with a hug, I heard Jacob scoff under his breath next to us.

'You alright, mate?' Oscar addressed him for the first time, a little tension setting over his body as I drew away from the embrace.

‘She hates it when people pick flowers,’ Jacob said. ‘Why let them die for three days in a vase when you can admire them where they grow for weeks?’

Oscar opened his mouth to speak, but I caught him before he said a word.

‘No, no, these are lovely. I love them, thank you, Oscar.’ Jacob shot me a look of both disgust and confusion. He was right, of course, he always was, but I couldn’t let Oscar know that, not when he’d made such an effort. ‘Jacob’s just a country bumpkin – don’t tell him about any trees being cut down because he’d be right there hugging it.’ I laughed, and so did all of my friends, albeit awkwardly. All except Jacob, who was now sitting perfectly still, only watching me with disappointment etched on his face.

For the next hour, the whole way around the exhibition, his expression remained unmoved, as though the wind had changed and it was now stuck like that permanently.

‘Jacob—’ I tried to catch him as he paced slowly at the back of the group, but Oscar and Freya jabbered so obstinately in my ear that I was constantly dragged away to hear more of Oscar’s sickly-sweet praise, or Freya’s random chattering.

He didn’t speak to me for the remainder of the art show. I didn’t get any congratulations or even a smile when we were presented with our top grade. Even the bus was too packed on the way home for me to get close enough to him to speak.

Instead, we stood, crushed like sardines in silence, trying not to fall into one another with each jolting stop.

'Jacob.' I finally had the space to call his name as the three of us reached our stop. 'Are you okay?' I had never seen him like this, so closed off, so rude. It was as if he had left his entire personality back on that platform in King's Cross and I had spent the day with a stranger.

Callum paced on ahead, always seeming to know the best times to make himself scares.

'Yeah, you know me,' Jacob said sourly. 'Just a country bumpkin overwhelmed by the bright lights and the fast pace.' A sharpness followed his words and they stung as they landed.

'I'm sorry, I was just trying to lighten the mood. You'd made them uncomfortable, Jacob. Those guys aren't like the people you hang out with at home. They wouldn't understand.'

'I do apologise. I must not have been taught any manners inside that barn I was raised in.' He scowled. 'I was telling the truth, something you apparently don't do down here.'

'That's not fair.' I sighed. 'I didn't want to hurt his feelings.'

'But you have no trouble hurting mine.' Jacob stormed off to follow Callum.

'What's that supposed to mean?' I went after him, but his legs only ever seemed to grow longer and he reached our flat before I could catch up.

Jacob maintained his quietness at dinner too. Mum and Dad had been busy working, so they'd left some take-away food on the side for us to grab. Usually on days like these, we'd eat off in our separate rooms, but since we had a guest, the living room sofa was good enough.

'How did it go?' Dad asked from the doorway, still dressed in his work clothes, tie and all, as though he hadn't had time to think about making himself comfy since he came through the door.

'Yeah, alright,' I murmured, and shovelled in a mouthful of noodles.

'Just alright?' he looked at me with furrowed brows, 'You've been excited about this for months.'

'We got an A+,' I added, hoping it would stop him asking questions.

'Brilliant.' Dad grinned, and scruffed the top of my head with his palm until I had to slick my hair back into place. 'And hello again, Jake. It's been a while – you've grown so much. How are you finding London?'

'It's pretty good,' he replied between bites.

'Gosh, you kids are just full of conversation tonight.' Dad shook his head, his eyes unable to hide the tiredness. 'You going to take Jake up on the roof and show him the view?'

I nodded. It was the thing I had been most excited to show him: my little hiding spot out of my bedroom window that was just high enough to make you feel like some supernatural creature, overlooking the city, keeping a watchful eye, and letting the world pass you by. It wasn't quite the treehouse, but it was close enough.

'You want to see?' My voice was quiet, timid almost, as I prepared for the rejection. When he nodded, the weight lifted from my chest and I mustered a smile for the first time since our argument. 'Come on.'

Following behind me, Jacob was silent aside from his controlled breaths. Opening the door to my bedroom, I hesitated for a moment before stepping in. My room was small, just big enough for a single bed and half a desk to work at. It wasn't like Hope Farm, or even Granny and Grandad's, where the rooms are so wide that even a dropped pillow made an echo. Everything seemed so homey there too. Each room had the Thorogood stamp on it, no surface was left unpainted or undecorated. My house, however, stayed in shades of beige, just in case we needed to sell it. I had my drawings pegged to a line of twine, not allowed to blu-tac the walls, or leave nails behind.

Jacob's words kept running around in my head: 'I was telling the truth. Something you apparently don't do down here.'

My life in London was so different to the life on the farm. And yet, I had no idea which version was the 'real' me. Were either of them? Was Jacob disappointed in London me? Maybe he only liked reckless, messy, fun Ava, when in reality, I was also city Ava – a girl with different friends and tidier hobbies. But the person I was that day, he couldn't even bring himself to smile at. It was only then, after I had seen him in my 'other' world, that I realised there was such a difference. It had never occurred to me before, in our summers covered in dirt, running wildly through the country, that when the holidays finished, things changed. Until then, I could be two different people with two separate lives, but with Jacob's arrival in London, I suddenly felt like I had to choose which was the real me. But I thought both were real. It's not like I was pretending, so why did I feel so fake?

'You okay?' he asked as we lingered in the doorway for too long.

Shaking my head and trying to dispel some of my thoughts, I pushed open the door wide enough for us both to fit through. 'Yeah, yeah,' I breathed, welcoming him in. 'It's not much. But it's home, I guess.'

Jacob took no notice of the lack of floor space or the shadowy walls. He headed straight over to my desk and skimmed his eyes over my drawings. 'How come none of these were in the art show?'

'I didn't even know you were paying attention.' I wasn't even trying to make a dig. He had just wandered around as though bored out of his mind. I'd barely seen him glance at my artwork, let alone notice which pieces I had or hadn't included.

Peering over his shoulder, I took a look at which one he was talking about. They were dresses I had designed for Granny – ones that kept hold of her signature style, full of colour and light, but they worked in compression garments, and added support for her as she struggled with her health. Then, beside it was the design I made for Lizzie's Christmas prom dress.

'Those ones aren't for show,' I said simply. 'They're too special, and no one can really appreciate how much they mean.'

'I do,' he said, putting them down and setting his sights on the window. 'The roof out here?' He didn't skip a beat.

Nodding, I unlatched it and hiked myself over the sill, and Jacob followed suit. Shimmying along the ledge, we finally came to a stop at a little square metre of flat roof space, just enough for the both of us to lean against the apex side by side and take in the view.

Sirens squealed, and cars revved their engines, but I relaxed into the sound, like a baby soothed by white noise. Jacob watched the city, and I watched him as he scanned the streets, looked out into the distance and stared into the abyss of the night sky.

'I like to come out here to think. You can see so much, it feels so wide, so open, not as cramped as everything else.' I spoke softly, unsure if he heard me over the traffic.

'There are no stars.' Jacob looked to me with sad, sloped eyes. 'No wonder everyone is in such a rush here, when there's nothing to slow down for. No constellations to get lost in, no sense that you are part of something bigger, greater.'

Jacob really doesn't fit into this life. I had thought perhaps him coming here would prove something to me, that we were meant to be something else, that we were something more than people who just enjoy one another's company when the holidays rolled around. Perhaps Jacob never really liked me . . . He just liked the farm, the adventure, the natural world, and I was just always there to come along for the ride.

'I wish I could send you just a few from back home,' he said. 'We have plenty, and that way, you wouldn't feel so far away.'

We sat with his words for a moment, letting the sound of the city fill the gap.

'You know, it's not that far away,' I spoke as though addressing the night. 'Just a couple of hours on the train.'

'It feels worlds away, though. I had always pictured in my head that you'd have a garden just like your granny's and you'd spend your weekends outside, just like you do back home.'

I looked at the little pot of petunias I had growing on the

roof that had wilted to nothing but soil, and the shame grew. 'You really hate it here?' My heart thumped in my chest, praying he'd say no, contradict me aggressively, tell me he was happy wherever I was.

'What? What makes you say that?' He furrowed his brows as though confused, but he knew exactly what I was talking about.

'It just feels like you'd rather be anywhere else today.'

'I'm sorry.' He sighed. 'It's just weird, because I didn't fit in with any of your friends. I couldn't be more different from them. And it just got me thinking, if you had the choice back at the farm, if I wasn't the only kid to play with when we met when we were eight, would you have ever looked twice at me?' A sad laugh escaped him.

I watched him from the corner of my eye. All I wanted to do was hold him.

'Don't be stupid. I'd have chosen you any day. I still would.'

'Even if I am just some country bumpkin that has no idea about the world, who can't keep up with your friends?'

'I'm sorry, Jacob. I shouldn't have said any of that. I didn't mean it.' I reached out my hand to take hold of his, and the relief when he didn't pull away settled my anxiety for just a second.

'I'm not sure what's worse. You meaning it, or not but still saying it anyway.'

I stayed silent, unable to defend myself, ashamed of myself.

'I'm sorry too. I was rude. I guess I was just so sure that I knew you better than anyone else in the world, and I was annoyed that I got it wrong.'

'I promise you, you do know me best.' I squeezed his hand tighter. 'I just don't think even I know who I am these days.'

'You and me both.' Jacob looked to me with a sad smile. I could tell from his expression that his thoughts were in as much turmoil as mine.

Perhaps he's thinking the same now – that we don't slot together as perfectly as we first thought. Maybe our real lives are just too different, that no summer romance, no treehouse fantasy, is enough to make us anything more than friends.

CHAPTER 21

Now

I stare at the ceiling of my room. The moonlight sheds just enough light on the Artex for me to follow its swooping patterns, in hopes that with enough time it might lull me into a sleep. I have no idea how long I've been lying like this, tracing the crumbling paint with only my eyes, trying not to think about everything, trying not to think about how we used to be before. But in telling myself that, my mind forces all of those thoughts to flood through me. How is it that I can be so exhausted, and yet my body just can't allow itself to switch off?

It's been a week since Halloween. A week of sleepless nights, ignoring everyone and all the notifications on my phone, and days crammed with work, just to fill my brain enough to not let me think any more about what happened. I am quite literally haunted by Halloween now. How ironic.

The first tap at the window, I pass off as the noises of an old house, adjusting to the cold of the end of autumn. The second tap, the same. The third, however, makes me stop for a second, listening for a fourth. Right on cue, it comes, and I watch the empty shell of a conker hit the pane of glass softly.

Shuffling out of bed, I wrap my dressing gown around me and look down at the garden below.

Jacob stands at the bottom, collecting the softest shells he can find at the foot of the horse chestnut, having not yet seen me. When he turns back and tosses the next one, I catch it in my hand, and fling it straight back at him, watching it as it bounces off his head.

'What did I tell you about my Granny's windows?' I whisper as he rubs the sore spot in his hairline.

'Sorry,' he replies, a guilty look crossing his face. 'It just couldn't wait.' His mouth shifts into a grin as he practically vibrates with excitement at the foot of the house.

'What couldn't wait?' I furrow my brows, intrigued, yet still trying to maintain my distance, reminding myself of all of our past meetings of late, my heart still sore from Halloween.

'Come down and I'll show you.' He beckons me, his smile entirely unreserved, his energy so infectious I have to stop myself leaping from the window just to join him faster. But I can't just act like I would have before. Has he just completely forgotten about our argument? Or is he happy with how we left it – agreeing that we are friends, nothing more?

'Or you could just tell me?' I whisper again, but the click of the bathroom light interrupts me and I force a hand over my mouth in hopes that I can dampen some of the noise. I stare at Jacob with wide eyes, putting a finger to my lips. He gets the message rather quickly and ducks behind the trunk of the tree, into the shaded edge of the night.

After a minute, once I've heard the footsteps retreat back along the hallway, I finally have the courage to speak again. 'Fine, just wait there and don't make a sound.'

Creeping around this old house is almost impossible. It's as though Granny and Grandad booby-trapped every floorboard and door to creak as loudly as possible to make sneaking out completely hopeless. As they both got older, it *had* become easier – either their hearing worsened, or they just couldn't be bothered to jump out of their beds in the middle of the night. But now that Mum is in residence, and she has insane bat-like hearing, I'm going to have to be smart about my escape.

The tree is a no go. My feet, and blood pressure, still haven't forgiven me from the last time. So, carrying my shoes with me, I shuffle along the landing on the very edge of each floorboard, making it to the stairs with hardly a murmur. Sitting down on the first step, I push myself over each one on my bum, hoping the extra surface area might balance my weight a little better, and I almost make it until the very last step—

The loud creak calls out to my mother like a snitching younger sibling, wanting me to get as far as possible to get into as much trouble as possible. Freezing, I hold my breath, hoping not a single exhale will be enough to push it and send mum's door flying open. When the yell doesn't come, or the aggressive footsteps, I race across the kitchen and out of the door before I dare take another breath.

Slipping on my shoes, I find Jacob exactly where I left him. He drags me by the hand out of the garden before either of us can make a sound. Once we are at a safe enough distance from the farm, I find my voice again. 'So what is all of this about?'

'Hope.' He grins, and takes me again by the hand, this time not stopping until we reach the barn on Hope Farm. Sliding open the doors, a small lamp is lit in the corner, casting a warm glow over a pile of hay. And there, in the middle of it all, Hope lies curled up, purring against two kittens that cry and mew through the first moments of their lives.

Turning back to Jacob, he watches me take it all in, my eyes growing hazy with each glance I make at the kittens.

'I thought she'd just been getting fat,' he explains. 'You know her age, coupled with the fact that you're here all of the time feeding her when you think no one has seen.' He laughs and I flush. 'But then she was making a proper racket earlier, and she's never been a cat to make a fuss, and so I followed her here, she got herself comfy, and then these two arrived not long after.' Jacob stands beside me now, as we watch the new family from a distance. Hope is unperturbed by visitors, and almost happy to show off her latest creations. 'I wanted to come and get you straight away, but I didn't want to leave her.'

'How long have you been out here?' I look at him in awe.

'What time is it?' he asks, bleary eyed.

'Just gone one.'

'Maybe four or five hours.' He shrugs, unable to stop admiring the kittens.

'Jesus, Jacob are you not cold? Or hungry?'

He rolls his eyes and presses his hand to my cheek, and the warmth of it spreads across my whole face in an instant.

'Clearly not.' I mumble, and tighten my dressing gown around myself.

For a moment or two, we stand side by side, simply observing in silence as two tiny creatures adjust to life on earth, completely clueless but leaning on each other to try and figure it out. Minutes pass like hours as we sit down on the hay, unable to take our eyes off the kittens as they cry out for their mother, who in turn licks at, and manoeuvres them, as their eyes still haven't opened.

The awkwardness of meeting again completely melts away at the sight of those kittens, and we sit side by side in complete tranquillity.

'How's the exhibition coming on?' Jacob asks after maybe an hour. His voice comes as a surprise, but I don't jump.

I thought he'd fallen asleep, propped up on the bale, but it seems he was just as transfixed as me, unable to fashion another thought while our minds were occupied with kittens.

'Not great,' I confess. 'It's like I sit down to do it, but nothing comes out. I scribble away at designs, or I sew some testers, and it's like my brain has stopped working. I tried to sew an entire dress with no bobbin the other day. The stupid thing fell to bits as soon as I picked it up. Pretty sure I'm losing my mind.' I laugh breathily, but there's no humour there.

'I can help you, you know, if you need it.' I glance at his face and he stares back with all sincerity. 'Me and Cal can give you a hand with some bits. I'm not sure how much help they'd be, but I know that even Alfie and Will would do anything for you. You know you only have to ask, right?' He's making sure to remind me that he is nothing more than a friend, the same as any of his brothers. I'm too tired to be hurt, and I know I shouldn't be. He's made it clear we're nothing more, and I have to respect that.

'You all have your own stuff,' I say. 'You don't need to worry about mine too.'

'I always worry about you.'

I lean my head against his shoulder, the tiredness filling my body, rendering me unable to truly absorb the weight of his words.

'I'll miss you, you know,' he whispers. 'When you're off on your adventure.'

'You'll *miss* me?' I can't bring myself to look at him. 'What about all of your adventures? Your photography, the farm, your animals. You won't have time to miss me.'

He does a little laugh, though it comes out as more of an exhaled breath that blows a streak of hair on my crown.

'You know . . . Me moving doesn't have to be the end of anything?' I say. 'I'll still visit in the holidays, just like old times.'

Finally, I sit up, and take in the whole of his face. In the dim light of the barn his eyes are glassy, a melancholy smile tugging on his lips. It's like neither of us wants to mention that I wasn't here last summer.

Friends, Ava. Just friends, I tell myself. *These are exactly the conversations that friends have at 2 a.m.*

'You are so much bigger than all of this, Ava. Bigger than the farm, than me, than this whole county. You'll go to Milan, you'll see the world, and you'll leave this place far behind. And I'll cheer you on when you do.'

'Don't talk like that. You're being silly now.' I huff. 'If you want to get rid of me, you can just say that.' A childish pout crosses my lip in my tiredness, and Jacob pulls me into his chest and I lie again, against his shoulder, fighting sleep with all of my might.

'I'm not ever going to forget about you,' I say sleepily, and his arm wraps around me tighter. 'How could I? You're my best friend.'

'I think it would be impossible for me to ever forget you,' is the last thing I hear as I drift into a deep sleep, lulled by his heart beat and the protection of his arm.

CHAPTER 22

Two years ago

There will never be a summer like the one you have at sixteen. At least, that's what my art teacher told me on my way out of my last exam.

We had nine long, languid weeks in the sun that year, when we didn't have a single thing to worry about between June and September. We were on the cusp of being grown up. Sixteen feels like you have the world on offer and all you have to do is reach out and take it, and yet, you're still kid enough to have Mum and Dad to fall back on, still naïve enough to enjoy it all without consequence. I could've stayed home in London if I'd wanted to, picnicking in Hyde Park, going to music festivals, or catching the train to Brighton and staying out on the pier until it's dark and we'd have to sprint to catch the last train home. But my summers had always been in the country. And though the last time I saw Jacob, when he'd come to visit me in the city, something wasn't right, I knew that everything would be okay once we were back to our familiar habitat.

'Are you sure you can trust him to drive?' I said to Jacob as we waited for Will to pick us up in his new car. He'd passed his driving test two months earlier, and had decided that we're to go in convoy to the beach. And though that sounds like a delicious idea because the temperature hadn't stopped climbing all week and I was desperate to wade in the coolness of the sea, I couldn't help but imagine all that could go wrong with Will in the driver's seat.

The Thorogoods had a tradition that every summer they'd spend at least a weekend at the coast, come rain or shine. Sian always said that if the sea air was good enough for sickly Victorians, it was good enough for them. And they were never too far away if they needed to be called back to the farm. This year, however, Sian and Dave had been so swamped on the farm that they hadn't found the time – it had been a tough spring that was shaping up into a hot summer, and they couldn't afford missing even a day.

I had always been so jealous when they'd disappear for the weekend. All my fun would stop, and I would sit alone in the treehouse wondering what they were getting up to. So, when Jacob mentioned heading out for the afternoon, just the boys and a few friends, I couldn't say no, despite my reservations about who was driving. This was my chance to get a little taster of the famous Thorogood beach weekend.

'You know he's driven a tractor on the farm since we were twelve, right?' Jacob had yet to mention anything about London, and neither had I. In all honesty, I was grateful. Perhaps he had just gotten up on the wrong side of the bed, or he was just a little overwhelmed with the travel and the city, but back home, everything continued as if his visit never happened at all.

'Yes, but I've also seen him try and jump a moped over a pig sty and end up with a face full of shit.' I chewed on my lip and clung a bit tighter to my towel.

Lizzie and Callum stood beside us, neither of them talking, just watching Lizzie's phone together whilst each of them let out a loud exhale from their nose at something funny, both of them completely unbothered at the prospect of climbing into Will's death trap.

'Okay, yeah, maybe he's not always been the most responsible, or the smartest. But one: he's got a black box so he can't go above about fifty miles an hour even if he wants to, and two: he's growing up a bit. The whole mardy thing he's got going on right now, it's because dad mentioned about him working full time on the farm, and now he thinks he's the man of the house.' Jacob rolled his eyes. 'Either way, I'll be right next to you, and if you get scared at any point, we will both get out and walk home if we have to.'

Just managing a smile, I thanked him silently for his

reassurance, and it didn't come a moment too soon. Will whipped around the corner in his Vauxhall Corsa and manually wound down his window to call out, 'Come on, plebs! The beach does await.'

I had always thought of the beach town as donkey rides, arcades that smell of old pennies, and eating fish and chips on the beach while you try to ignore the fact that your paper is full of sand and the seagulls are circling. And it is all of those things, in the best possible way. But Will, in his surprisingly tame driving, took a little detour just up the coast to a quiet spot away from the screams from the sea-front rides, to a section of beach that seemed like no one else knew existed.

Okay, maybe after five too many pot holes hit at full speed, I did end up clutching Jacob's hand in my own sweaty palm, and then had to awkwardly peel myself off of him, but he didn't seem to mind.

Another two cars, packed full of faces I vaguely recognised from Halloween parties past, and Alfie, were already there when we arrived. Will, after Jacob reminded him to put his handbrake on, was the first to leap out of the car, greeting his friends and fussing about how many disposable barbecues to take down to the sand, and who was the strongest friend to carry the cool box that was apparently stuffed with meat.

'Right, his driving was enough, but he's going to be cooking too? I've seen enough of his barbecuing at Halloween parties to know that's a hard pass from me'. I pulled a face at Jacob and he broke out into a laugh.

'You really have no faith in him, do you?' He chuckled. 'Don't worry, I don't either. I packed us some sandwiches.'

'Cheese and pickle?' I grinned.

'And a prawn cocktail crisp garnish, of course.'

'I could kiss you!' I patted him excitedly on the thigh and he blushed through his laughter. Before we could fall into an awkward silence, my door swung open, the sunlight flooded the car, and I had to squint to see the person behind it.

'Adam!' I only needed to see the shock of red hair to remember him from the last Halloween party. He kept me company through the night whilst everyone around us got a little too drunk, and he had been very punctual with texting me since. 'How are you?'

I climbed out of the car to meet him, and I was grateful for the wide expanse of his rugby player shoulders as he shaded me from the beating sun.

'Better, now I know you're here and I'm not just stuck with all this lot.' He pointed to his friends that had already started to wrestle in the thin layer of sand that covered the car park.

'Honestly, I've been questioning why I agreed to this before I even got in the car,' I said, shaking my head. I glanced back into the car for Jacob, but he must have climbed out the other side and had disappeared into the mass of testosterone.

'Well, I, for one, am glad you did.'

I flushed. He'd been this flirty over text, but guys always seemed to have the confidence behind a screen but could never back it up in person. Adam, however, was seemingly an outlier, and I'd be lying if I said I wasn't a little too flustered to reply.

'Here, let me get those for you.' Adam took my bag, towel, and shoes that I'd slipped off as soon as I had seen the sand. I thanked him softly, still struggling to find my voice.

'Right everyone! Grab a bag, and let's go,' Will ordered the crowd as self-appointed leader, then scarpered down a dune and out of sight. Jacob followed closely behind him, not noticing the hand that I raised to ask him to wait up. Callum and Lizzie sauntered off with Alfie, as they always did. I had no choice but to stick with Adam, and, in all honesty, I wasn't complaining.

After a little trek through some fenced off dunes and an amble through some overgrown shrubbery, it began to make a little more sense as to why this beach was so secluded. But with each incline and decline, Adam offered me his free hand – the other was still laden with all of my bags – and made his best effort not to let me fall. We were the last to arrive at the camp, as conversations about his rugby team and my fashion projects took priority over our speed. The barbecues were already lit by the time we reached the others.

Finding a spot next to Jacob, I sat down beside him, and Adam beside me, as our conversation didn't even pause with the change of location.

'I'd love to study in London, always have,' Adam said. 'You're so lucky that it's literally just your norm.' His face glistened with a coating of sweat, and he glowed delicately in the sun, the rays turning his red hair into strands of gold. 'And it would be amazing to do a year or two aboard too. Somewhere in Europe, maybe.'

'Ugh, yes,' I promptly replied. 'I've been looking at some courses in Italy, and the South of France. Imagine leaving your lessons and then you just get to cycle your way through the most beautiful cities on earth.'

'Why would you want to spend all that money and travel so far for something when you could do just the same back here?' Jacob butted into the conversation with his pessimism, and I was reminded of his attitude back in London.

I prickled. 'The world is a far bigger place than this beach, or even London. If you actually let yourself try something new for once, you might realise how much is out there.'

'Or, if you appreciated what you've actually got, you might not feel the need to want to run off every chance you get.'

I narrowed my eyes at him as the tension hardened between us.

'Jesus, Jake. You sound like you need a beer, mate.' Adam tried to diffuse the pressure between us that was threatening to implode, but Jacob only rolled his eyes. He debated whether to say something for a moment – I could see his lips twitching as he tried to compromise with his conscience – but he eventually decided against it. Instead, he got to his feet and moved to another spot in the circle. He landed beside Pen, who, of course, had brought her guitar. They soon fell into a conversation that he clearly liked better than mine. It was only when he caught me watching them that I realised I was still unable to wipe the sour expression from my face.

Adam talked at me for another little while, but all I could do was watch Jacob and Pen as he made her giggle. He seemed to have a hell of a lot to say for a man who had always been too shy even at his own dinner table. What could he be saying to her? Why was she laughing like that? He wasn't that funny – not funny enough to warrant the leg slapping and the cackle, that's for sure. When he opened his bag and offered her *my* cheese and pickle sandwich with prawn cocktails crisps, which she had the audacity to reject with an upturned nose, I fought every urge to stamp over the row of barbecues like a hot coal walk and throttle him.

As the sun began to set and I was suitably fizzling in the sand, Alfie took his moment to mix things up a little, as he always seemed to do.

'Truth or Dare!' He announced to the group, gesturing to each of us with a burnt hot dog pinched between his fingers.

A few members of the party groaned while the rest sat up a little straighter in anticipation.

'Will, you're first,' Alfie decreed, and his oldest brother swiped his hands on his shorts in preparation. 'Truth or dare?'

Of course, Will chose the latter. I couldn't imagine him talking about any of his feelings or secrets, so dare was by far his safest option. Alfie tapped his chin for a moment, undoubtedly deliberating what he could force his big brother to do that would both torture and humiliate him. 'Eat that sausage.' He pointed to a victim of Will's grilling skills that ended up flicked off the coals and into the sand, where it had lain collecting a sandy coating for at least the last hour.

Without a second thought or any worries about the ten-second rule, Will scarfed it down as though he hadn't just eaten six, and all of his rugby friends, including Adam, cheered when he flashed his clean, if a little sandy, mouth to the crowd.

Callum opted for truth – again, unsurprising – and he confessed to having to go to the toilet in an old World War Two pillbox. I remembered this; it happened when we were fourteen after we walked a little too far once and he'd eaten a dodgy takeaway pizza the night before. Needs must, I suppose.

Charlie, another one of the boys' mates, picked dare, and had to down an entire bottle of beer in one go. It was gone in seconds with a roaring belch to finish it off, which of course elicited a loud reaction from everyone. Lizzie went dare, and she had to stick her whole head in the sea and pull out a piece of seaweed using only her teeth. She completed rather successfully without even a second thought. As the game went on, two more of Will's friends did dares, one involving an uncomfortable degree of nudity and another eating the seaweed Lizzie had pulled out.

'Jacob, truth or dare.' Alfie shoved the sausage of doom in his brother's face and Jacob rolled his eyes. 'Truth.'

Alfie, obviously hoping to command his other brother to do something ludicrous, looked a little disappointed for a second, until a menacing smirk crosses his face. 'When are you going to grow a pair and tell Ava you're in love with her?'

For the first time all day, everyone went deathly silent. The sound of the waves crashing to shore grew louder and louder as we waited a lifetime for an answer. If the group's eyes weren't on Jacob, they were on me, burning with excitement for the gossip, or awaiting a moment of heart aching rejection. My heart rattled in my chest, and I wanted nothing more than to stand up and wade out into the sea and hope Poseidon swallowed me whole.

Jacob rolled his eyes after far too many beats of silence, and shook his head with a laugh. That alone was enough to sting, but his words were excruciating. 'There's nothing between us. She's my mate, just like Callum, and I'm not in love with him either.' His words were rushed, but I heard them loud and clear. Callum didn't laugh at this joke either. He just looked at me with a sorry expression and tried to smile, but he looked about as pathetic as I felt.

'All righty.' Alfie too was a little lost for words. He tried to shift the attention to a new victim as quickly as he could. 'Pen. Truth or Dare.'

'Truth.'

'Who do you have a crush on?' Standard, easy – low risk, high reward.

'Jake.' She said it with a nonchalant shrug and blinked up at him expectantly. I didn't think he'd heard her at first – he was sitting there with an absent look on his face as though he was in deep thought, but I couldn't bring myself to watch them any longer.

I all but tuned out the game until my own name was called. Deciding that there had been far too many emotional confessions about matters of the heart that evening that had only left me feeling like a fool, I chose dare, hoping that Alfie might dare me to walk home, or just disappear into the night.

'I dare you . . .' Alfie thought for a moment, then smirked. 'To kiss a person of your choice in this circle.' My eyes flicked to Jacob, who was already looking at me, a dark expression clouding his eyes. He'd humiliated me, and been nothing but an arsehole this evening. He'd confessed to almost everyone he knows that he didn't like me, that I was nothing more to him than a 'mate', no more special than any other person sitting in this circle.

So, I had not an ounce of hesitation as I turned to Adam and raised my eyebrow. As soon as his head twitched in a nod, I clasped him by the face and pressed my lips to his with such force that he had to steady himself by anchoring his hand in the sand. Whoops and cheers went up around the circle. As I refused to do anything by half, I practically stuck my tongue down his throat, and Adam returned the favour with the same level of passion. My phone vibrated in my pocket, and I finally pulled away. Adam and I were both flushed and panting.

'Ava Matthews!' Lizzie looked at me with wide eyes and a look of pride slapped across her face as she whistled in respect.

Adam only stared at me, stunned, but I couldn't bring myself to stay sitting beside him. Getting to my feet, I began to wander back along the beach alone. Adam started to follow me, but I was grateful when he was distracted by Alfie daring himself to run off into the sea completely naked. I could hear the group cheering him on into the cold water.

'Why are you following me?' I didn't need to turn around to know the footsteps in the sand behind me belonged to Jacob.

'Where are you going?' he fired back, increasing his pace to try and catch me as I neared the dunes I recognised from earlier.

'That's none of your concern.'

Jacob reached me as I tried and failed to scramble up the sand and instead ended up sinking into it until I lost my balance and fell to my knees.

'Don't touch me,' I snapped as he held me by the arm to help me up. I shook myself out of his grip as soon as I felt his fingers on me.

'Ava,' he said sternly, though a little hurt seeped into his voice.

'No, Jacob. You don't get to do this – make me feel like shit, and then just pretend like nothing's happened. I ca– can't keep doing this all the time. You're messing with my head and I don't want to play this game any more.' I let him take a step towards me, but I still couldn't bring myself to look him in the eye.

'What game? Ava, I'm not playing any games.' He tried to pull me closer, to move my face to force me to look at him, but I clung to my strength.

'So why are you so hot and cold? Why is it that one minute

am I the centre of your bloody universe, and the next I'm hardly even your mate? How is it that we can spend hours alone feeling like we're the only two people in the world, and the next, you can't even look at me?' Finally, I stared him down, my eyed filled with tears, but my face was so stern, so unrelenting that he faltered for a second. My phone vibrated persistently in my pocket, but I couldn't bring myself to look at it, too charged, too angry to let this argument waver for even a moment.

Jacob ran a hand up his face, and he tugged at his hair with his fist as he tried to scramble for some words. 'You—you're upset because I didn't tell all of Will's mates that I'm in love with you?'

'No, Jacob! I'm upset that you came all the way to London, and acted like I was a stranger. You wouldn't talk to my friends, you didn't care about my art show, you looked like you wished to be anywhere else. Then you acted like nothing was up, before switching up on me again on the beach. I can't keep up! I don't understand what's happened to you.'

Though we'd spoken about it, and even though he'd apologised, I still hadn't managed to shake London from my head. He made no effort to attempt to go out of his comfort zone, he had no open mind about coming into 'my' world. No, it's like he assumed I'd always just fit into his small world.

'What's happened to *me*?' He scoffed, his face so close

to mine I could feel his breath fan across my cheeks. 'Ava, you humiliated me in front of your friends, you *lied* to all of them. I came all the way to London to have to watch you cosy up to some pretty boy, accepting his flowers, and now you sit there and get off with some lad you've known for five seconds. I have no idea who *you* are any more.'

'*I* humiliated *you*?' The words sit like milk gone bad on my tongue as I spit them back at him. 'You talked about my dreams as though I was a fool for even imagining that that could one day be my life. That just because I don't want to spend my life in the same place I've grown up in, I'm wasting my time?' I shook my head and stared him down. 'And you don't get to say a single thing about Adam when you sat there all night, all over Pen. Why even follow me when it's clear you were hoping to get into her pants tonight?'

Jacob laughed, and shook his head. My phone buzzed loud enough for us both to hear and I fought the urge to lob it across the sand and leave it for the sea to wash away in the next tide.

'You couldn't be more wrong.' His words dripped with venom, before he softened a little, and I could tell his heart was breaking. 'Every chance you get, you remind me I'm not good enough, that all of this is not good enough.' He had to clear his throat as it thickened with his emotions. 'I am not, and I *never* will be enough for you. I'm just some kid that lives on a farm and is going nowhere, while you have the whole world at your feet. You're waiting for something more exciting to come along, when I'm just waiting for you. You coming to stay is the only thing I look forward to, I live for those few days, or few weeks. But to you, I'm just some village idiot with no dreams, no wild aspirations. You have no space for me in your great plans, Ava – I've known that for long enough now.'

He took a step towards me, and I watched as his chest rose and fell rapidly with each of his heaving breaths. Instinctively, my hands went to his chest, but I couldn't work out whether I wanted to push him away or draw him closer, so I held him there, feeling his heart beat pummelling against me.

'But I'm just your "mate". Why do you care?' I whispered.

Jacob took another small step towards me and took my wrist in his hand. He was so close I could feel the heat of his body radiating against mine, as each of his breaths pushed him closer into me. I was pulled to him, my eyes drawn to his lips, my body only a hair away from his. He pressed his jaw together, and all I wanted to do was to sweep my finger along his chin and feel him relax into my touch. I wanted to press my lips to his, to twist my hand through the waves of his hair, to feel his hands on my body.

'Ava?' Callum's voice came panicked through the darkness. Jacob drew away with an almost pained inhale of breath, and

I whirled around to look for my brother, my heart knowing just from the sound of his voice that something was wrong.

When I reached him, his whole face was wet. His sweat had smeared with his tears until he looked like a vision of pain, illuminated by the moonlight. Before he said anything, he ran into me, locking his arms around me in a desperate embrace, like a child recently woken from a nightmare and needing to cling to the good of the real world.

'Callum, what's happened?' I searched his face, my heart thumping so aggressively that the motion made me feel sick.

'Mum's been trying to call you.' My stomach dropped. 'It's Granny.'

He didn't have to say any more, just shake his head, and I collapsed into him. We both tumbled into the sand, clinging to each other so tightly as the world fell down around us.

The drive back to the farm was completely silent. Callum and I still clutched each other, crying silently. Will kept his eyes firmly on the road while Lizzie shivered, staring wide-eyed out of the window, unable to stop her own tears. Jacob sat pressed beside me, his pinky finger pressed against the side of my thigh to remind me he was there.

When we reached the farm, we didn't say goodbye. Callum and I rushed in to find Mum sat at the kitchen table, her head in her hands. At the sound of our entry, she looked up, tears lit by the lamp linger in her lashes. She tried her best to smile, but before her lips could make a curve, she broke down into sobs.

Callum glanced at me before moving beside her and placing his hand on her shoulder.

'I'm so sorry, kids. She's gone.'

CHAPTER 23

Now

'That has to be the last one, surely?' Callum asks – practically begs – as he sets down another box of my designs, sweating from the weight of the pile of cotton.

'Nope, there's two more,' Jacob answers for me as he comes in behind my brother, also weighed down by the masses of fabric he's carried from his truck. Rain drips from his hairline and runs down his face but every single one of my pieces remains bone dry, as his coat is spread over the top of it.

'Surely, you're not going to fit all of it at this tiny table, Ava. Jeez.' Callum looks at the modest set up that is supposed to be big enough for me to prove my worth as a designer – supposed to carry the weight of my future in fashion. I'm crammed into a small corner of the marquee they've set up in the town park with only a picnic table and two cork boards to fill. I've definitely gone overboard.

'I thought it would be best to have plenty to choose from. I keep changing my mind on what I need to include. I don't know if I should emphasise the technical elements, or overall design.' I pace up and down the length of the table, tugging at my hair, hoping that any new sensation might kick my brain into gear. 'Plus, how can I know what looks best against this backdrop without trying various combinations?' The rain still hammers at the canvas marquee, each drop drumming through the space and filling me with dread.

'Ava.' Jacob takes my hands in his. 'You're going to be perfect. Stop overthinking it. You've done all of the hard work, now all you need to do is let everyone else see how brilliant you are.'

He holds me for a moment longer, raising an eyebrow as he awaits a reply, and when I reluctantly nod, he smiles, releases my hands, and paces out of the tent again to fetch the rest of my things.

Things have been strange since the night in the barn. We seem to have finally agreed on it out loud – that we're friends. Best friends. But I fell asleep on his chest that night, and now he's holding my hands. Does he do this with all of his friends? Would Pen be okay knowing what has passed between us? Where is the boundary? If I wasn't so freaked out about this exhibition, maybe I'd be worrying about it all a little more, but right now, all I can focus on is which of my twenty designs, if any, are good enough to display.

'He's right, you know.' Callum speaks up as he lifts one of

the dresses that I made for Granny's funeral out of the box. He can't pull his eyes from it. 'You've got a real talent Ava, and anyone with eyes will be able to see that. As much as I don't want you to leave me and move across the continent, it's where you belong, and no matter what happens here, you'll get there.'

Tears well in my eyes. Callum has never been a typical brother – he's always been kind, not the sort to tease me or pull my hair, but hearing him talk like this still feels like a novelty.

'Cringe,' I squeeze out past my tears and push him softly on the shoulder. He only shakes his head and smiles before he, too, turns away to fetch the last box from the truck.

The wind flaps under the edges of the tent, its cold breath whipping at my ankles and wobbling a few of the tables. The rain doesn't give up either; the thumping on the canvas only crescendos until the quiet mutterings of the other artists putting their exhibits together is almost completely drowned out. I falter at every step, second-guessing each pick and placement, but the boys steady me – in turns reassuring and stern, especially when I dally for too long on a particular decision.

Despite it all, however, the three of us soon add the finishing touches to the display, with all of my designs framing the centre title 'Granny's Garden'. Floral fabrics cover the table, along with photos of my inspiration in the eponymous garden, and the ones of Granny at her machine takes pride of place at the focal point of it all. Designs that marry beauty and femininity, with practicality and medical accessibility, fill my table and dress the mannequins on either side. For the first time, I can honestly say I'm proud of myself.

'It's perfect.' Callum grins.

Jacob nods and wraps an arm around my shoulder. He doesn't need to say any words, he presses me tight into him and that's enough for me to know he's proud of me too.

'Come on, let's go and get something to eat.' I take them both by the hand and give them a grateful squeeze, before we try and brave the elements.

Racing back across the park through the rain, we're soaked by the time we reach Jacob's truck. With each passing moment, the little bit of bad weather teeters on the edge of a raging storm. From this distance, we watch as the marquee gets battered from every angle, the wooden stakes clinging on for dear life as the rain turns the ground to mush.

Lightning forks across the dark sky, fracturing the thick blanket of clouds and officially earning its amber weather warning.

'It will be alright, won't it?' I chew my lip as we drive away from the park, the tent still in my sights. All the bodies that filled it before flee from inside and race to find shelter in their cars or nearby cafes.

Jacob looks at me in the rear-view mirror and gives me a reassuring smile. 'Those marquees are designed to withstand all kinds of weather. I'm sure it will be fine.'

Famous last words.

Storm Brenda rattles through the county for the rest of the afternoon and into the evening. Though her name would suggest a sweet older lady that would give you fifty pence to 'treat yourself', no trampoline, no wheelie bin, no ginormous tents are safe in the mouth of her wrath. Even the treehouse shakes with her wind, and all I can do is watch from the window as the rain slashes against the earth and darkness engulfs the day.

The council posts a photo of the aftermath the following morning. The exhibition is a wash out, with pieces of art littered across the boggy park, and my mannequins are three inches deep in mud, as though they've just crawled through No Man's Land.

So, after a cry, and a lot of swearing, I find myself in the kitchen of Hope Farm to continue my sulking. I was hoping to find Jacob, but instead, it is Lizzie and Alfie I must turn to for sympathy. I have been complaining to them loudly about all the hours I put into the work, though I don't mention that all that hard work also helped me avoid people and places I didn't want to think about.

'Bit of a stupid idea putting on an exhibition in a tent in November, though, isn't it?' Alfie mutters. Lizzie shoots him a look so black it makes him hold his hands up in surrender. 'I'm just saying what everyone's thinking!'

Lizzie looks as though she's about to argue with him, but she must realise he's making a good point as she shrugs and turns back to me.

'They'll be salvaging your actual dresses though, won't they?' Lizzie tries her best to comfort me as I groan over the breakfast spread.

'I don't know. There's probably nothing left worth saving.' I shove a croissant into my mouth in hopes that the buttery pastry will at least numb the pain for a little while, but it only ends up flaking all down my top and irritating me even more. 'All my hard work down the drain.' The more I think about it, the more it hurts. This was my last shot of making sure my place in Milan is secure, and now it's ruined. How am I meant to start my fashion coursework from scratch this late, by myself? There's no way I'm getting a passable grade after all this.

'Can't you just make some more?' Alfie says with his mouth full. Lizzie and I both death stare him this time, and he takes that as his cue to leave us alone.

'Where's Jacob?' I had assumed he was simply sleeping in,

but as the day itches closer to noon, I begin to worry a little.

'Oh, he went out really early this morning. Didn't say where he was going.'

Probably with Pen, my pessimistic mind suggests in an attempt to keep my mood at its absolute lowest.

'You know, the dress you made me for prom . . .' Lizzie begins, uncharacteristically seriously. 'That was the most confident I've ever felt. You've really got a talent for this, Ava.'

I know she's only trying to make me feel better, but it's working. I muster just enough warmth for a smile. 'Thanks Lizzie, I'm glad.'

'Would you make my wedding dress for me?' she asks with full sincerity.

'Have I missed a chapter or two?' I reply with a nervous laugh.

'No, no, I just mean if it ever happened. I'd like you to make my dress.' She grows bashful, which is very much unlike the woman that has beaten up Alfie Thorogood and won since she was five years old. 'We might be old ladies by then, but I don't think I'd want to get married at all unless it was in a dress that you made.'

I stick out my little finger in her direction. She takes it in hers and squeezes tightly. 'Then,' I promise, 'even if I'm eighty and can't even see my pins and needles, I'll make your wedding dress.'

'Erm, sorry to interrupt.' Will coughs from the door awkwardly. 'But I think you might want to see this.'

CHAPTER 24

Two years ago

Granny always loved embroidery; she'd spend hours with her glasses perched on the end of her nose, stitching away at her intricate designs. But as she got older, her fingers lost their strength, and all of her designs lost their little details. When I asked her one day why she didn't just buy an embroidery machine, where she wouldn't have to use her hands or rely on her failing eyes, she looked at me a bit perplexed.

'I don't sew because it's convenient, or easy,' she said after a moment. 'I sew because every single thing I create has some of me in it. When I see you wearing your dresses, or your costumes, I see my pricked fingers, and my strained eyes, but I also see that dress as time – time I spent on you. You may come here every summer, and pop in in the holidays, but when you're not here, I still spend my hours with you, stitching the fabric in a way I know won't tickle that spot on the back of your neck that always makes you itchy, or in a pattern in which I know you can be a princess that also gets stuck far too often in the mud. Every time I sit down to embroider, I think of you and your brother. Anyone could make a t-shirt out of this fabric, but not everyone has a t-shirt that they know someone made with love, that they can look at long after I'm gone, and feel like they still have my time.'

That was when I realised her own clothes never had embroidery like mine. She didn't have castles on her hems, or flowers on her sleeves. She gave everyone else her time, her art, but no one ever returned the favour.

I couldn't help but think of that as I faced her wardrobe. It was an explosion of colour, as though stepping into it would transport you, not to Narnia, but somewhere warm, where the sky was always blue, and flowers grew even through winter.

Granny hated wearing black. Even to the funerals of her friends, that felt like they came almost monthly, she always made sure to wear a colourful scarf. 'Everyone deserves to leave this world getting to see the colour of life,' she used to say. She knew full well that dead people don't see colour, but I think it made her feel better. Sitting in rooms shrouded in black must've got tiring, bleak, but that pop of colour gave her a little hope. Her scarves were hung up on the inside of the wardrobe door, like a rainbow waterfall.

She'd hate that we're wearing black for her now.

'Oh, Ava.' Grandad shuffled into the bedroom with his shoulders hunched. 'You scared me, duckie,' he said quietly as he sat down on the edge of his bed, following my eyes to her wardrobe. 'She always looked so beautiful, didn't she.'

Granny and Grandad had always had enough love between them for the rest of us. Sure, Grandad used to tease Granny like crazy – he'd make fart noises when she'd sit down, or pretend to be asleep in his armchair every time she'd ask him a question, or hide her glasses under the tea cosy – and yet with every tut and shake of her head, she'd always let her grin slip through. When Granny got sick a few years earlier, his humour didn't change, at least not in front of her. He took the tea cosy to her bedside at the hospital, just to hear her laugh again. Back home, however, was when you could really see how he loved her. He kept every inch of the place spotless, awaiting her return. He fretted in the kitchen by a phone he didn't know how to use, waiting for word.

He looked utterly lost without her. He still does, even still now.

I'd cried so much those last few weeks that I couldn't summon the energy for more tears, but his words made my eyes sting. Unable to fashion a reply, I could only nod, still facing the wardrobe, too afraid to look at him.

'Look at this one.' He picked up a photo frame from his bedside table. I'd seen it a thousand times. When we were kids, we'd sneak into bed with Granny and Grandad for a story and a cuddle before bed. The photo was of Granny and Grandad in their younger days, maybe thirties, just smiling together in the farmyard. It was simple, just two people in love, surrounded by the place they call home. That time, I took note of what she was wearing. It was a baby blue dress that floated across her body as though she had plucked a cloud from the sky and fashioned a skirt from it. The chiffon sleeves fell over her arm in a gentle caress on one side, and a breeze gently lifted the other. 'She made that dress herself. Made me a matching tie with the fabric.' Grandad smiled sadly at the memory. 'They're both still in there.'

Sliding through the rail, I felt each fabric against my fingertips, all of them soft, all of them natural, all of them felt like they'd be a privilege to wear. I found the dress near the end, and plucked it out from the others, running the material across my hands until the little hairs prickle.

'You can have it,' Grandad said, pinching one of the sleeves between his fingers and lingering, as though remembering the way it felt when he held Granny all those years ago.

'Are you sure?' I whispered.

'Everything in there is yours. Your Granny always made sure to tell me that.'

'Thank you.' We sat side by side for another moment. The memories we were both replaying in our minds of her would have been different, I'm sure, but our situation was the same: we'd both lost the most important woman in our lives, and the idea of navigating the future without her was terrifying.

For the next week, I sat in the treehouse alone, embroidering Granny's dress. I took the photo too, to 'spend time' with Granny as I worked. My fingers burned with each stitch, and my eyes were so blurred that I could hardly see at some points, but still, I threaded flowers up and down the skirt until the whole thing was covered in a garden of embroidery. My tears darkened the fabric with every fallen drop, but after a little while, they disappeared and didn't stain. I told myself each time that it was Granny, there with her hanky, blotting them away and fussing that if I didn't stop soon, she would have to stick it on a boil wash.

A plate of sandwiches slid across the floor of the treehouse towards me, and I stabbed my finger with the fright. Jacob's head popped up behind it, and my heart rate quickly returned to its comfortable state.

'What's this about?' I eyed him and the sandwiches suspiciously. I had seen him only in passing since we got the news about Granny. The Thorogoods were the first ones around with dinners packed into Tupperware and sorry faces. But I had hardly spoken to anyone in weeks, either shutting myself away in my bedroom to cry, or hiding in the treehouse, desperate to do something to bring me just a little bit closer to her.

'You need to eat,' he said gently, inching the plate closer still.

'I'm not hungry,' I murmured, afraid his kindness might set off my crying again.

'You've been up here for six hours, Ava. You need to look after yourself too, you know.' I didn't ask him if he'd been watching me. My traitorous stomach answered him for me and groaned loud enough for both of us to hear.

Taking one of the triangles, I thanked him with a smile, and he took that as an invitation to slide across the treehouse to sit beside me, and take one for himself.

'Is that the same dress?' he remarked, looking at the picture of Granny and Grandad. I nodded. 'It's beautiful.'

We were silent for a little while longer, not needing conversation, just needing the company. It was almost dark by the time I found my voice again.

'Will you come?' I spoke, hoarsely. 'To the funeral I mean.'

'Of course I will. I'll always be there. Why wouldn't I?'

'You've always hated wearing suits. I remember distinctly you saying you'd "rather jump in the slurry pit than wear that many layers".'

Jacob laughed softly and shook his head. 'Hey, I said I'd be there, I didn't say what I'd be wearing.' He nudged me gently with his shoulder. 'You have nothing to worry about, Ava.' Seriousness took over once again. 'I'll be there for you; we all will. And we'll be there for Granny. And you only need to give me one look, and I will whisk you right out of that church, and we will finally disappear into the wilderness.'

I believed him. I believed every word he could ever say.

The last time we were alone together like this, we were at each other's throats on the beach. But none of that mattered any more, at least not right now. Adam, Pen, all of our childish jealousies and gripes meant nothing in that moment, forgotten temporarily as something far more important took precedence. It was like we'd settled into an unspoken truce. Maybe we would argue about it again another day in the future, but all that mattered was that regardless of how angry we were with one another, he was here when I needed him most. No words spoken before then were more important than my best friend supporting me through the worst days of my life.

Jacob did come to the funeral. As I climbed out of the car in my powder blue dress that was covered from bust to hem in hand-stitched embroidery, he waited for me outside. His suit was perfectly pressed, his trousers reached his ankles, and his tie was almost an exact match of the one Granny made for Grandad.

It was then, I knew, I could get through that day.

CHAPTER 25

Now

'Will, no offence but I'm really not in the mood to give you a hand with fixing your tractor, or hosing down any cows.' I groan as I trek behind him, dragging my feet in the gravel.

'I'm going to just pretend you didn't say that.' He pauses briefly to place a hand on his chest, offended, before resuming his break-neck pace that leaves Lizzie and I practically jogging.

Ironically, the day is beautiful. The only traces left of storm Brenda are a few little puddles along the driveway. If it weren't for the fact that I can see my breath as I walk, I wouldn't blame anyone for thinking this was the blue sky of a spring day. The farms are quiet this time of year – the animals are in their sheds, the winter fields are drilled, and a sense of calm settles on the place. Today doesn't feel like that, though.

I hear their voices before I see them. Will guides us around to the treehouse where a crowd has gathered. Freya is always the loudest one in any group, and it doesn't take me long to pick her out, alongside Ash, and Oscar.

'What's going on?' I turn to Will, but he only gives me a menacing smile. 'Is that my *dad*?' I ask, already knowing full well that it is. He's standing next to Dave Thorogood, nodding and chatting away as though he's been here all along. I hadn't realised how much I missed him until I see him here, grinning from ear to ear, completely unchanged from happier days.

Freya, pausing in her conversation long enough to notice me, rushes over to pull me into a hug. 'Look at this place! How exciting!'

'What are you doing here?' I must be dreaming. I look between my friends, then to Mum, who is standing next to my Dad for the first time in months. They both look actually happy to be together again, as they hang out around my childhood treehouse. I can only stare at Freya perplexed. My heart feels full, and I rub at my eyes wondering if this is all real. Maybe a stray tree branch, loosened by storm Brenda, had actually knocked me out last night and all of this is some sort of hallucination. Either way, real or not, this is the first time I've felt whole in weeks.

Looking past the array of familiar faces, I notice they're all gathered around something. Ribbons wrap around the branches of the tree, and photographs are pinned to the trunk the whole way up until you reach the treehouse, and that too has been decorated with fairy lights and draped with fabrics. For the first time I see Jacob, stood as far up the tree as he can get, smiling down at the scene below like some angel admiring his divine work.

'Nice to see you too.' Freya shoves me by the shoulder before squeezing me tight in her embrace again. 'Jacob invited us,' she says, wiggling her eyebrows. 'All the trains were cancelled in that freak storm, but your dad saved the day. Drove us all here in the early hours.'

'But what for?' I'm still perplexed, my mind unable to catch up with all of these new events that have been thrown a me.

'Well, we came for your exhibition. But obviously, that didn't go to plan with the whole flood and mud thing, so here we are.' Freya pulls me towards the tree so I can see more clearly. Photographs of costumes, of Granny, of my work, cover nearly every knot and knoll. 'I think he salvaged what he could from the mud and a few of his own bits, and brought the exhibition home to you instead.' She nudges me again, wrapping herself around my arm to look at me with her dreamy eyes that only ever suggest one thing.

One of the photos is of Will, Jacob, Alfie, and Callum, all styled with skinny scarves, plastic high heels and a couple of tiaras: the first fashion show I ever directed. I had swept the whole barn and lined the catwalk with bales of hay and forced all of the boys to dress up while Lizzie took photos on Jacob's camera. They pretended to hate it, but their struts and twirls said otherwise. Most of these other photos I've never seen before. Many of them are of me through the years, but there are also ones of Granny, the garden, the treehouse, of the very same exhibition we set up yesterday that no one saw but us. Every single one of these photos was taken by him, in moments of silent observation, and he's done all of this for me.

Searching for him, I'm pulled in every direction as Oscar and Ash call my name, Sian and Dave clap me on the shoulder to congratulate me, and Alfie hands me a photo he's plucked off the tree. It's of himself when he was seven years old, and I had dressed him up in an outfit that makes him look like an extra out of *Bridgerton*, if they all wore plastic top hats and jackets sewn by an eight-year-old.

Sidestepping him and his grumpy pout, I slip away to find Jacob, who is no longer among the tree's branches. My heart is pounding in my chest. He's done all of this, for me. He's taken all of these pictures, developed them, for ten years. He's captured my whole life here on camera, without me ever even noticing. And above all else, he's brought everyone here, my two lives woven together in this moment, and it all seems to slot together perfectly in a way I could never imagine before. I need to thank him. I need to throw my arms around him, I need to—

'Ava!' Pen calls from across the field as she joins us all late. 'This looks amazing! I'm sorry I'm late. I hope you don't mind, but I brought Mrs Hill from your photography class.' She leans a little closer. 'I think it's a lovely idea from Jake, but I figured you'd still need that little bit of extra credit from her for uni, so we might as well make the most of what he's done.'

Why does she have to be so bloody perfect?

'Thank you, Pen. Really . . . thank you so much.' I clutch her by her hands and she gives me a wink, before taking Mrs Hill on a tour of the treehouse.

'It looks like I don't need to ask how you're settling in up here.' Dad finds me catching my breath for a moment. As he looks around at the spectacle with such a soft look of pride, I could almost be convinced that he was about to cry.

'I've missed you.' He pulls me in close and I bury my face in his shirt.

'I've missed you too. Thank you for coming all this way. And for bringing all of those guys – I know it can't have been the most peaceful journey.' Dad and I chuckle together as we watch Freya talk the ear off of Sian Thorogood, who can only nod to keep up with her.

'Ava, you know you only have to ask, and I'd be here in a flash. Just because me and your mum aren't together any more, doesn't mean we can't both be in your life.'

I smile sadly at him, unable to find the words to respond.

Mum wanders up behind me and squeezes me by the shoulders, planting a wet kiss on my cheek. 'So proud of you.'

Then she turns to Dad and places her hand on his back as naturally as she's ever done. 'Could you ever imagine that we could make two humans that are so brilliant, eh?'

'You guys don't have to pretend that everything is okay, you know,' I mutter. 'I'm not a kid any more.'

Dad smiles and shakes his head. 'Whether you like it or not, you and your brother will always be our babies.' He pinches my cheek like he used to when I was younger. 'I know it doesn't feel like it right now, but things aren't not okay, Ava. Me and your mum both realised that our priorities were all in the wrong places. Hell, you're going to university next year, and this is the first exhibition of yours that I've ever been to. We both worked too much, we both lost ourselves and each other thinking that we were making a good life for you kids, not realising that we were only making it worse.'

'We could have all moved together.' I feel like a child, calling out for Mum and Dad in the middle of the night after a nightmare.

Mum speaks next, her brave face slipping away in favour of genuine confidence. How have I not noticed that that's what she's been trying to hide? 'Sometimes, we have to let things go. They hurt in the moment, but you realise that in the long run, that loss is the only thing that can make your future a happy one. I'll always love your dad. But we're both happier now. And I hope one day you'll realise you are too. Look at all of this Ava.' She points to the mob around the tree. 'You're going to be just fine, wherever you go.'

I hug them both tightly, and they wrap their arms around me and each other. It suddenly clicks for me – they're both in a better headspace. Despite Dad's early morning taxi services to my friends, the dark circles around his eyes have cleared, he looks well rested, his hair is neatly cut, his face freshly shaven. Dad doesn't look anything like the version of him we left in London a few months ago. He looks happy.

Maybe Mum didn't break his heart. Maybe she didn't rip a hole in this family. Maybe if she'd waited that year longer, both of them would be past the point of return. Catching a glimpse of her, I notice for the first time that she too seems brighter, less tired, more in tune with herself and the world around her. She excuses herself to go off and chatter away to everyone, not once letting her smile slip, but I know this one is genuine.

It still hurts. But maybe they're right; maybe all of this will be worth it in the end.

'Well Miss Matthews, I have to say, you get points for originality. Can't say I've ever had to climb a tree to do my marking before, but here we are.' Mrs Hill chuckles to herself as she taps her Biro against her chin. We're standing at the periphery of the group that has gathered, and the mingling of my London life and farm life seems to carry on just fine without me. 'I know it is not your original plan, but I'm impressed.'

'I need to confess something.' Her bushy eyebrows sink under her glasses. 'None of the photos are mine, they're all taken by Jacob. Mine were ruined in the storm. I'm grateful you're here, but I can't accept this as my grade for photography.'

Mrs Hill cackles, and the abrupt noise makes me jump. 'I know it's all Thorogood. I've been familiar with his work for a while now – the style he has is something of a marvel. But you forget I am also here because of your fashion A-level. I have been in touch with your tutor back in London after you gave me her details, and she has given me the authority to look at your work and send her my thoughts ahead of your final course work grading. I've taken plenty of photos for her to cross reference, but it is all looking in tip-top shape to me. You should have nothing to worry about, Miss Milan.' Sliding her glasses back up her nose, she walks back across the field and out of sight. 'Cheerio!'

I can only take a moment to blink and absorb all of this. All hope for my future, it seems, is not lost.

Pen watches on from the side, her hands clasped together in genuine happiness. Sucking in a deep breath, I finally find the nerve to approach her. 'I need to thank you,' I say. 'I really don't know how I can repay you.'

'Don't be silly, that's what friends are for!' She smiles, and my gut gurgles.

'But I haven't been a good friend to you.' The sight of her now, looking so genuine, so kind, makes the guilt from my feelings eat me alive.

'You mean about Jake?' she replies without hesitation.

I nod, too ashamed to speak. Have I been that obvious?

'Me and Jake aren't together. Not any more,' Pen says. 'To be honest, I don't even think you could say we were in a relationship, not properly anyway. We'd only really hang out in the group, but I think we were mostly together because we were both lonely.'

'I don't understand?' I shake my head, unable to comprehend what she's telling me. I've seen them together. I've watched them embrace. For years.

Pen curls her lip in a sad smile, not like her usual cheery self. 'I wanted us to be together, but I don't think his heart was ever in it. We gave it a go a couple of times, but it's hard getting a guy to love you when he's already in love with someone else.'

I open and close my mouth, trying to find something to

say, but no words come through.

Pen just chuckles. 'Yes, I mean you, Ava. Since you came back, I tried to make it all work, but it was never going to happen. That night you saw us in the treehouse . . . he was calling the whole thing off. For good.'

'But—the Halloween party?' I mumble out loud, though I doubt she has any idea what I'm referring to. If he *had* split up with her then, why didn't he correct me when I confronted him about having a girlfriend? Why would he still insist we were friends if he left her because of his feelings for me? My brain throbs in my skull, and I have to rub my temples to try and relieve some tension.

'I don't know what happened then, but he's a confusing boy, that's for sure.'

For the first time in the years of knowing her, she has a genuine sadness cloud her face and I pity her. 'I'm so sorry, Pen.' Behind her confidence and her beauty, she's been a real person, caught in the middle of all this messiness. Part of it is my fault, but I also know all too well how much a heart broken by Jacob Thorogood hurts.

'It's my fault. I should have run far away after our first break up, when he first told me he liked you as more than a friend. But I had always just hoped that one day, he might feel just a fraction of what he felt for you for me. I was jealous of the way you've always been each other's favourite person.

I've never had that, and I realise that I'm not going to if I keep trying to cling to Jake. He's a good friend, he always will be, but that's all.'

There's too much to digest there. The first time they broke up? When did Jacob tell her he liked me? And if she's always been jealous of me, the same way I have been of her . . .

'Why would you help me?' I can't help but ask. 'Why bring Mrs Hill? Why would you be so nice to me when I've done nothing at all to deserve it? Why not scream and cry, and pull my hair?'

Pen only laughs a weak, resigned laugh. 'None of us can help who we fall in love with.'

I open my mouth to apologise again, but she places her slender hand on my shoulder and smiles, genuinely this time. 'It's sad, beyond measure, and it would probably be easier to hate you, but I don't.'

With no words left that would be of any use, I wrap my arms around her in a tight embrace. She's a better person than I could ever be. 'Thank you, Pen.'

CHAPTER 26

Two years ago

Pops of colour littered the barn as Granny's favourite songs filled her wake. She had all of this planned out – down to the little cocktail sausages and mini scotch eggs that she'd never be able to have a buffet without. She had planned it long before she got sick; I suppose it was her way of having a bit of control over the inevitable. But really, I think she planned it all so Grandad wouldn't have to. He'd hardly slept for weeks, so not having the pressure of making these difficult decisions had been a godsend. Plus, I reckon she wouldn't have trusted anyone else. No one would have filled this place with as much joy as she could, and though everyone was yearning to be sad, and to mourn, her playlist ensured that everyone must stay on the dancefloor.

Jacob and I danced together, swaying to the songs Granny used to hum around the farm without knowing the lyrics. I let him hold me, the heat of his touch kept me upright, kept the tears at bay for another moment. His own eyes were still bloodshot from the church. He loved my Granny as much as his own, and I know she loved him too.

'Your dress really did come out perfect,' Jacob said lowly as

I spun around and my skirt fanned out against him.

'Where did you get the tie from?' I hooked the silky material in my finger and felt the length of it. Jacob smiled.

'My dad has about six blue ties, but none of them were the right colour. I had to get Will to drive me over to Lizzie's place so I could steal one off of my uncle. It's not exactly the same, but it was as close as I could get.' The sight of that little blue strip of fabric had kept my head above water all day. Even as we danced, I couldn't be too sad so long as it was in my eyeline.

'It's perfect.' We fell back into the rhythm of the song and danced until our feet hurt and we had to retreat to the chairs for a rest. Callum, Lizzie and the other Thorogood brothers weaved in and out, sometimes keeping us silent company, other times reminiscing about Granny – her biscuits, the way she muttered when we dragged mud around the house, or our favourites among her creations.

When all of the guests had retired, and the buffet was tidied away, Jacob and I lingered for a little while longer, savouring the last moments until our goodbyes were done, clinging onto this day as though after this, we had to accept that she was really gone. All of the Thorogoods walked back with us to Grandad's house, with cards, flowers and food tucked under their arms, proving yet again that they really are more like family than just neighbours.

When Dave had washed all of the dishes left from the night before, and Sian had run around with the hoover, they said their goodbyes and the six of them crossed the farm again to head home. With Mum exhausted, and Callum in no mood to be sociable, Grandad and I sat alone together at the kitchen table. Not a word passed between us, but it was clear we both needed the company.

'There's a box in the top of the wardrobe,' Grandad finally spoke after a while. 'I'm not sure exactly what's in there – I haven't been able to bring myself to look – but I thought maybe you would.' He kept his eyes fixed on the wood grain of the table, tracing the swirls with his finger.

'Thank you.' My voice was almost a whisper and he nodded.

'I wish it was me, that went first.' He shook his head. 'Your granny would've been able to cope better on her own. It was always her that knew what to do. For fifty-five years she kept me going, and now I don't know how to live without her.'

Tears fell freely down my face as his voice cracked.

What could I say? There are no words in the English language that can comfort a man who has just lost his whole world. For half a century, he'd spent every day with the woman he loves. After that long, they were no longer two individuals, but two halves of one whole. Grandad hadn't just lost his wife; he had lost himself too. How are you meant to start over again in your seventies?

Knowing there was nothing I could say, I embraced him instead. Grandad has never been the hugging type, but he didn't protest as I held him against Granny's dress and let him soak it with his tears. We stayed like this for a while, until he had no tears left to cry, and he excused himself to bed for an early night.

When I followed behind a few minutes later, I found the box outside his door. It was an old Clarks shoe box taped on the corners and overflowing. Unable to leave it undisturbed, I tiptoed across the landing to pick it up. I couldn't take it to my room; there was only one place that felt right to open it in.

I scurried across the garden in the dark of the night to climb the treehouse.

As soon as I slid the batteries into the camping lantern and bathed the treehouse in light, Jacob appeared like a moth at the window.

'Were you sitting up waiting for me?' I asked. He was still in his suit, tie loosened and shirt untucked.

'I knew you'd not be able to sleep and end up out here eventually. You're earlier than I predicted, though.'

'Creep.' I shook my head and tried to hide my smile in the shadowy edge of the treehouse.

'What you got there?' Unbothered by my comment, he

gestured to the box and shuffled into his normal position beside me.

Instead of telling him, I opened the lid. Out of it spilled piles of letters stacked together with photographs. Jacob scooped a few of them up and sifted through them with the same look of intrigue that I felt.

'Look at this!' He turned a sepia photo towards me. It was of Granny and another woman when they were young. Grandad stood off to the side, his arms folded, looking suitably grumpy.

'That must be his sister.' I chuckled. 'The photo must have been taken before he'd confessed to his feelings, back when they hated each other.'

'They hated each other?' Jacob asked as though he couldn't ever imagine that being true.

'Apparently. According to Granny.' I shrugged and picked out my own photo of the two of them kissing on their wedding day, Granny almost completely obscured under her layers and layers of lace. 'Although, looking at this, it's clear that didn't last long.'

There were love letters that dated right back to the sixties, filled with my Grandad's scrawled handwriting, kept perfectly neat, without so much as a wrinkle or a tear. These were her prized possessions, that much was clear.

'Imagine being loved this much,' I commented, tears of

joy clouding my vision for a moment as I went back and forth between letters, photographs, old cinema tickets, and scraps of fabric that will have meant more to Granny than they look here.

'They really have lived a perfect life.' Jacob's voice was soft, as though he was somewhere far away and this was all a dream.

After laughs and tears, I took a break from Granny's memories for a while to watch the stars from the window. They scattered across the night sky in their silvery clusters. Though there are millions, each one was just as sublime as the last.

'It's getting late,' I remarked absently, noticing the chill of midnight seeping through the gaps in the treehouse. 'I should head back. Try to get some sleep.'

Jacob looked up from the box of photos. The one in his hand, one of Granny and Grandad's wedding day where her skirts jutted out so wide that grandad's short arms had to stretch out just to hold her hand, made him smile as he showed it to me.

'Just five more minutes?' he asked, his eyes pleading.

'It's cold.' Though I shivered, I didn't want to leave, but the longer I stayed, the harder it would be.

'Come here.' He opened his arms for me to crawl into. He pulled his suit jacket off and wrapped it round my shoulders as I came closer, then pulled me into him. He was warm-blooded to the core, and even in the harshest of cold snaps, he always seemed to throb with heat.

I couldn't refuse. I tucked myself beside him as he pressed his body to mine. The cold was long forgotten as soon as his body pressed to mine and I flushed with warmth. My heart thronged with an erratic beat in my chest. As he looked down on me, his dark eyes looked almost black in the low light of the camping lantern.

'Thank you, Jacob.'

'What for?' He scanned my face as though I was his night sky, and every last bit of me had to be savoured as there was no one part more worthy of his attention.

'For today,' I said simply. 'For every day. I think you're more of me than I am. Having you by my side makes me feel whole.'

That smile. The one filled with crooked teeth, and blushed lips. The one he reserved only for me. That smile put the very moon to shame as he beamed at me. When he slid a hand across my cheek and it settled in my hair, our shaking breaths aligned, until we trembled against one another. The other hand found its way to my waist, his usually warm touch sending shivers around my body until I pulsated beneath him.

When he pressed his lips to mine, I was home. They were

the only part of his body that felt cool, but their touch set me alight from the inside.

His mouth, his touch, the fire throbbing through me made me realise that until this moment, I had never been complete. I had never known what it is to be whole, until Jacob Thorogood had kissed me.

CHAPTER 27

Now

'Are you hiding from me?' I find Jacob in the barn, clutching both of Hope's kittens in his hands as their mother slaps a bit of hay across the floor. 'Your mum invited everyone back for dinner, but we couldn't find you anywhere.'

'*You* found me,' he observes.

'I always do, eventually.' I meet him in the middle of the room, and he hands me a kitten. The thing is hardly bigger than my palm, and she sits against my chest purring away from the heat. 'You didn't answer my question.'

'I'm not hiding from you.' He doesn't look up from the kitten that's fussing in his hand. 'Like you say, you always find me, so hiding from you would be pointless.'

I take a few steps towards him, my breath trembling with each passing second. 'I wanted to thank you, Jacob.' I say, placing my hand on his arm, and forcing him to meet my eyes.

'What for?'

'What for?' I roll my eyes. 'For saving the day? For inviting everyone from London? For all of those photos? What you did . . . I never even thought someone could be so thoughtful. I was so ready to just accept defeat and give it all up, but you gave me a second chance, and that second chance was better than I could have ever hoped for. And those photos, Jacob – so many years of memories that I thought I just had to cling onto in my own mind – they're the best gift. They're priceless, and I really don't know how I could ever repay you.'

Jacob's eyes find the floor again and he takes a breath before he speaks. 'You don't need to thank me. That's what friends are for.'

The words form a vacuum around us to steal the air from my lungs and stop my heart.

'Friends?' The question comes out of me deflated, hardly even voiced at all and full enough of my heartbreak for me to not need any other words.

Surely, we are more than that. There is no way this is all the act of a 'friend'. What about everything Pen just told me? She said it herself, they're not together – he ended things with her because of his feelings for me. And what about our late nights and the years of almost confessions? All those times I have fallen asleep in his embrace? What about all of the almost kisses, in the orchard, on the beach, or any place that we've been left alone in for long enough? What about that damned kiss in the treehouse that we've both pretended never happened? Are those the words and actions of a *friend?*

'I'm sure if Freya was here, she'd have done the same. Or Oscar,' he continues. Why is he continuing? Why isn't he finally falling into my arms? Why aren't we getting our happily ever after? Why are we all still pretending?

'No, they wouldn't, Jacob. They wouldn't.' I can't summon any strength in my voice. It trembles in a pathetic whisper as I bite back the tears.

I step closer to him, reaching out for him, but he turns away, sets down the kitten, scruffs Hope on the top of her head, and mumbles something about being late for dinner before leaving the barn without looking back.

My own legs, however, have no strength in them to follow him. Collapsing onto a hay bale, I let myself cry freely and sob into the palms of my hands.

'Mum's looking for you guys,' Will's voice calls. 'You need to get some food before—oh.' His interruption comes too late as he finds me alone and breaking.

The hay beside me shifts with the weight of another and I blink through the tears to see his face. Will places an awkward hand on my back in a way that would imply he's trying to comfort me, but he thinks that if he presses too hard, I might crumble, or turn on him. I've certainly been known to do the latter a few too many times, so I don't blame him for his fear.

'Do you need me to punch him?' he whispers after a few more awkward minutes rubbing my back like I'm sick at a party after a few too many drinks.

I try my best to laugh, but it just comes out as a damp,

snot-filled breath. Shaking my head, I try and swipe away the moisture on my face, but still the tears fall. 'I really . . . I just thought we were more than friends.' I sniff. 'Was it really just nothing, all this time?'

Will sighs. I can't work out if it's out of sympathy, or regret that he bothered to get himself involved, but he gives me a tight smile that looks more like a grimace, and finally pulls his hand away.

'All I know is that I've never seen him like he was after you left the last time. Whatever fight you had then really did a number on him.'

'Wait, what?' I swipe at my face aggressively, as though wiping away my tears would help me to hear him better.

'I don't know what you said to him, but man, it broke his heart.'

'*I* broke *his* heart?' I remember that night so vividly. Still, I wrack my brains for anything I could have said, any way I could have hurt him, but I'm only reminded of my own pain.

'I don't think I saw him for days,' Will explains. 'Usually, he's like an animal, happy to wander the earth alone, but always comes home for food. But no. That summer, after your Granny's funeral, he just disappeared. He came home a few days later, and then didn't leave his room, as though it hurt more to be outside. It took weeks for him to tell me it was because of you, and months before he went back to any sort of normal. Mum hasn't let him out of the house without a phone since. We were all worried sick.'

I don't understand. Jacob wasn't the only one suffering from sleepless nights. For weeks after that, I could hardly function. I'm not sure I even remember the days after that night in the treehouse. It's like my mind switched off and I kicked into auto-pilot, knowing that any more heartbreak might send me spiralling. *He* was the one that left me there that morning, alone.

'He was the one that made his choice,' I say to Will, confused.

Will's face mirrors mine, brows furrowed, head tilted just a little to the side as if nothing I just said registered in his brain as English. 'I don't know . . . he seemed pretty gutted if it was his choice.'

My head aches from all of this back and forth. I have flicked through so many emotions in the space of half a day that I'm sure one more word from anyone will be enough to make my skull explode. Massaging my temples with my thumbs, I try my best to make sense of it all: Jacob's actions, his words, my conversation with Pen, Will's revelations. My throbbing heart is being pulled in every direction and at risk of being torn into several pieces.

'What am I supposed to do, Will?' I plead with him, my tears flowing anew.

Instead of answering, he pulls me tightly into his chest, burying my face in his shirt, not worrying about me soaking it. Will has never been one for words, but on rare occasions, he's given the best hugs – even if it's just to muffle your sobbing after one of his ideas for a game has gone wrong and he doesn't want you to run off crying.

'Just don't give up,' he murmurs as my crying settles. Getting to his feet, he rubs his hand across the top of my head, sending my hair into a static mess, before walking away as though none of this ever happened.

CHAPTER 28

Two years ago

I'm sorry

That was all he'd left behind for me. I knew his handwriting; I'd know it anywhere. He never left enough space for an apostrophe; it was always crammed between the letters that were pressed together in his joined-up style. When we were kids, I asked him how he did it – managed to join every letter seamlessly – but he had shrugged and said he only did it because he's too lazy to lift the pen from the page. There was no denying that this lazy scribble belonged to him.

My hand trembled as I read those two words over and over. The ink smudged as my tears hammered the page. There must've been some sort of mistake.

Climbing down from the treehouse in a daze, I found myself in the yard of Hope Farm, desperately searching for him, hoping I'd find him making me a flask of tea and he'd explain that it was all a misunderstanding.

'Ava.' An unexpected voice found me before I reached his home.

'Adam?' I pressed my palms into my eye sockets to try

and clear the tears, and to make sure I wasn't hallucinating. When his red hair pulled back into full focus, the confusion knocked me out of my anxious stupor for a moment. 'What are you doing here?'

'I needed to catch you. I wouldn't forgive myself if I didn't.' I hadn't seen him since that night on the beach, and so much had happened since then that he'd hardly crossed my mind.

Seeing him now, so serious, stirred a sense of dread within me. 'What's going on?'

'I came by last night to see Will and had no idea that you were all having the wake for your Gran. I'm so sorry, by the way.' He cringed at his own heavy handedness, but it didn't deter him. 'I hung around for a little bit, at Will's request. He had some bits he wanted to show me on his car – but that's irrelevant. Anyway, I saw how close you were with Jake . . . and I thought you deserved to know.'

'Know what?' I could've shaken him, but still, he chewed on the inside of his cheek, debating how to tell me.

'After the beach, where, you know, we kissed—'

'Yes?' I pushed him on, my patience dangerously thin.

'Well . . . Jake got together with Pen after that night. And, well, they've been seeing each other ever since. I'm sorry, Ava.' With every word, he held my gaze, his eyes showing no hint of deception, his face carrying the guilt of telling me.

I shook my head, slow at first and then harder, and harder

still until I could hardly see him standing in front of me. 'No,' I said sternly. 'No, it's not true.' He wouldn't do that to me, not when he knew what I was going through with Granny. Surely?

'He's with her now, Ava. I passed them on my way here,' he persisted, but still, I shook my head.

'If you're telling the truth, then prove it.' My voice warbled.

Adam sighed. 'Are you sure?'

I nodded furiously.

Digging his keys out of his pocket, he gestured to his car and got into the driver's seat. He looked at me nervously as I climbed in beside him.

'Let's go,' I urged, and he turned on the ignition and drove the small stretch of road to the village. I was too anxious to speak, and he was chewing on his lip like he didn't want to do this.

'Ava . . .' Adam started but he tapered off as they came into view.

Pen and Jacob sat opposite one another around a small bistro table at a café that looked out across the village. The very same lips that kissed me only the night before, chatted away to Pen unreservedly, as though he was unable to control himself in her presence. Those fingers that caressed my skin, now fiddled with a wooden stirrer. It was the nervous fidgeting of a man in the presence of a woman who turns his brain to mush and sends his heart thumping. Those eyes that cried with me, that smiled with me, gazed upon her after abandoning me with only one measly note, scrawled with two pathetic words when I had been praying for three.

I couldn't bear to look any more. My eyes fell to my lap, and the tears fell against the skirt of Granny's dress that I had yet to take off.

'I'm sorry, Ava.' Adam's voice was almost a whisper, and I was grateful that he took my silence as permission to restart the car and drive me home again.

'You don't have to be sorry.' I finally spoke, gaze still fixed on my own quivering fingers. 'You're the only one who's had the balls to tell me the truth.' All day yesterday, Jacob had sat with me, danced with me, and lent me his shoulder to cry on. How could he not have told me he was dating Pen? That he had been for weeks?

'I wish I wasn't the one that had to make you cry, though.' Looking up, I tried my best to flash him a reassuring smile, but his sad eyes still sloped in a way that made him look almost equally heartbroken.

Pulling into the driveway of grandad's farm, Adam dropped me off with another sad smile.

Mum was in the kitchen when I made my walk of shame. I tried my hardest to sneak past her, but as soon as I took a step, she whipped around. 'Are you okay?' she fussed instantly, gliding across the kitchen to look at me closer.

'I fell asleep in the treehouse looking at Granny's photos.' It wasn't a lie, and it was enough to explain the roughness of my appearance, but Mum still looked at me with a raised brow. I was grateful when she didn't push any more.

'Are you all packed for our drive?'

I'd almost forgotten that we were meant to go back to London today. Normally, I'd fight, beg for just a few hours longer, get us delayed enough that Mum would complain about driving in the dark. But that day, I nodded defeatedly. 'I'll be ready soon.'

'Will that give you enough time to say bye to all of your friends?' Her suspicious gaze didn't drop as I nodded once again without any conflict or resistance. 'All right then, darling, you go and get yourself a bath and get packing.'

Mum always knew when to not bother with questions. She knew she would get nothing out of me in this state, but I also knew I wasn't out of the line of interrogation. I was sure I'd be grilled in a few days, but by then it wouldn't be so raw. I leaned down to kiss her on the cheek and excused myself to the bathroom.

Climbing into the bath, I let it fill around me until I disappeared under the water, and the warmth flooded through to my bones.

The Jacob I thought I knew was gone. That's if he ever existed at all.

After an hour in the bath, the events of the last few days finally sunk in. I had no more tears left to cry, so I washed my face, and scrubbed every pore of my body until I felt almost human again. Maybe this was for the best. Lizzie, Alfie and Will would understand if I didn't say goodbye – they would know I'm still upset after Granny. And this way, I wouldn't need to see Jacob or talk to him again before we left.

I hadn't realised then that I would avoid him, and the countryside, for two years.

CHAPTER 29

Now

'You're up early.' Mum's voice startles me as I reach the kitchen. The morning is still dark, and she sits in her pyjamas at the dining table, shrouded in the warm glow of a lamp. 'Are you sneaking out again?'

'Again?' I almost choke, but Mum only chuckles.

'Ava, I've been a teenage girl living in this house. Anything you've thought of, I tried it twenty years ago.' She winks and I flush. 'That bottom step always gave me away too.'

'I wasn't sneaking out . . . I couldn't sleep.' I plonk myself down beside her and notice the old Clarks shoe box she has open in front of her. 'Granny's photos?'

Mum nods. 'I haven't been able to bring myself to look at them, but then I saw those ones that Jake took for your exhibition, and, well, I thought I'd give it a go.' Her lips find a sad smile before she gets to her feet. 'Cuppa?'

I don't need to reply, she already knows I need one. So, she flicks on the kettle and we both listen to it simmer. A few wedding photos are on the top of the pile, and there's a damp smudge still on the corners from where Mum had been looking at them only moments ago. I saw the contents of this box inside out two summers ago, but the feeling I get while looking at each photo is unchanged from the very first time.

'I wish I had spent more time with you all here in the summers,' Mum says as soon as the kettle clicks and she has an excuse to turn away from me under the pretence of making tea. 'By the looks of things, I missed out on something rather special.'

I nod, but realising she can't see me, I hum. 'I'd trade years of my life to have one more summer with her.'

'Me too.' Mum sets down my tea in front of me and returns to her seat with a long breath. 'I had hoped that us moving here would give you just a little bit of that feeling. I'm sorry if I was wrong.'

I pick up a photo of Granny standing beside Callum and I. We're dressed like two field mice, and she proudly shows us off to the camera. 'You weren't wrong. I just don't think any of us quite realised how much of the magic was just Granny.'

Mum holds up another photo. 'I think you might be right.' She places her hand on the table beside mine and presses her pinkie finger against me. 'Although, I reckon she passed on some of that magic to you.' She nudges me gently, then glances at the photo in my hand. 'I didn't realise how quickly you'd grow up. I know you asked me why I didn't wait another year—'

'I'm sorry, Mum,' I say quickly. 'I was angry and I took it

out on you and—'

'I understand, Ava. What I was saying is that I brought us back here now, so we could have at least one more year together. Who knows when we'll all be back in the same kitchen again? With you galivanting across Europe and your brother burying his head in his books at uni, I only have one year until you both really are grown-ups, and I wanted to make sure I didn't waste a second of it.'

I lean my head against her shoulder. 'It was nice to see Dad. He seems happy. Happier than I thought he was.'

'We both are.' Mum combs her nails through my hair. 'And I'm sorry that you're not.'

'I don't know how I feel any more.' I confess and I feel her chest deflate with her breath. 'Do you still believe in love? Even though you and Dad didn't work out?'

'Of course, I do,' she says without hesitation. 'I loved your dad for over twenty years, and I still do now. I don't regret any of the time we spent together.' She hesitates for a moment, as if unsure how to say the next part. 'It was out of love for each other that we had to let go of our romantic relationship. We love each other, but love changes, and sometimes the best way to love someone is to let them go.' Just like Granny used to do, she strokes me by the hair and all of her words settle on me softly, as though deep down I knew them all along. 'I may be going through a divorce, but I'm surrounded by love now, more than I ever was before. I have you, and Callum, and your grandad. We all still have Granny, in our hearts, our memories, and in the very seams of our tops and trousers.' She slides out another photograph. 'Do you not believe in love?'

'I don't think so,' I confess. 'I think maybe Granny and Grandad were the exception.'

'Because of your dad and me?' She ceases her caresses and looks at me with a pained expression.

'Jacob.' His name comes out in a whisper, and Mum sighs and holds me tightly.

'Oh Ava.' She doesn't ask, but I tell her anyway. I tell her about Pen, and the treehouse, the kiss, and the note. I cry when I tell her about his rejection yesterday, and she holds me closer still when I tell her that I have always loved him.

'Anyone with eyes in the last ten years can see that boy feels something for you,' Mum says into my hair. 'I may not have been around much, but I was around enough to see that. I don't think you should give up on love just yet.'

'He doesn't love me, Mum. He's made that clear.'

'Didn't Granny ever tell you about how she got together with Grandad? They had years of misunderstandings and missed opportunities.'

'I haven't got any more time for missed opportunities. I'm moving away in less than a year. We've missed our chance.

Plus, Jacob has never sent me letters like these.' I take the heap from Granny's box and skim through the masses of papers, all filled with Grandad's raw confessions. And all I'd gotten from him were two words: *I'm sorry*.

'You have your whole life ahead of you. Moving to Milan is the beginning of your whole life – you don't need to let that stop you from being in love. Love is bigger than any country; it will travel with you. You don't have to leave it behind.'

As she speaks, I run my finger along each letter, seeing Granny's name printed in the same handwriting over and over until I stop dead in my tracks. My name interrupts the wave in scrawled, joined up writing. Hesitating for a moment, my fingers hover over the sheet, too afraid to touch it, as if any contact at all would set it alight and turn it to ash before I can read the letter's contents.

'I think Granny might still be working a little bit of her magic, after all of this time.' Mum stands up and takes her mug of tea with her. 'I'll leave you to it.' She winks and closes the door behind her.

CHAPTER 30

Now

Kitty,

I have spent years trying to find the words to express how I feel about you, and now that you lie snoring on my shoulder, I think I'm finally ready.

Just saying that I love you doesn't feel like enough. How can three words be enough to tell you that every time I'm with you, you make my heart pound so wildly that I can hardly breathe? And yet at the same time I never feel more at peace? 'I love you' can't explain how I only ever truly feel like myself when I'm with you, as if all I am in between those moments is just a man without a soul, and a boy without a dream. Telling you I love you doesn't touch the surface on how much I need you when you're not here. Those words aren't vast enough to explain to you that I don't even feel human when I'm with you, Ava. I'm an animal, whose only instinct is to stay by your side.

But I do love you. I love you, Ava Matthews. I have loved you since we were eight years old and you couldn't climb a tree without getting a splinter, and I could hardly form a sentence in your presence. I couldn't explain it then, but I felt it. I have never not felt it. A decade of friendship has turned this into a love that I know will last for decades more.

I have made all of the wrong decisions, I let my jealousy blind me, let my fear of losing you get in the way of it all, but please don't tell me I'm too late. If you'll have me, I'll apply to finish college with you in London. I would move to the edge of the world if it meant I could be closer to you. I would sleep on that tiny patch of your roof, under a starless sky, just as long as I knew I'd see you when I woke up.

I'm going to put it all right, Kitty. I'm going to fix my mistakes. I promise.

If you feel for me even half of what I feel for you, meet me back here, in the treehouse, before you have to leave.

I love you.

Yours always,

Wolfie

My chest heaves with the weight of my breaths. I feel like I am collapsing in on myself every time I read another word. That letter has sat in that box for two years. Two whole years, he has thought I rejected him. Two years I have wasted.

I refuse to waste any more time.

Still clad in my pyjamas, I leave my shoes at the door as I race across the fields through wet grass and cold mud. The sunrise glows amber across the horizon, but I don't stop to admire it. The barn is my first stop, but when I swing open the door, there's no one there, apart from Hope and her babies who yelp at sun in their eyes.

Sprinting into the yard of Hope Farm, it's Will I find first, yawning on the bench as he pulls on his boots.

'Where's Jacob?' I pant.

'Good morning to you too,' he grumbles, his voice hoarse from his early start.

'Where is he?' I rush, too impatient for his grouchiness.

'Jesus, he's in the orchard.' Will yawns again. 'He's been getting up early and heading down there.'

I rush, grabbing his keys from the bench beside him. 'You mind if I borrow these?'

I don't wait to hear his reply as I hop into his tractor and strike up the ignition. I've seen Grandad drive his Betty, and I have been in this cab with Jacob so many times. How hard can it be?

Will swears loudly as I pull out of the farm, but he doesn't bother to chase me down. The tractor hums across the fields until the orchard comes into view, but even with my foot to the floor, it isn't fast enough. Abandoning the machine in the middle of a boggy pasture, I run the rest of the acre to him until the mud hits my knees and I am heaving for breath.

Jacob doesn't notice me at first. He sits in the back of his truck, watching the sunrise across the orchard, as the last of the autumn sun fills the gaps in the trees.

Picking up an apple that had been forgotten in the harvest, I throw it just hard enough to hit the back of his shoulder and burst into a juice against his shirt.

'What the—' Jacob turns around, ready to fight back, but when he spots me, his face softens and he waves a nervous hand in my direction.

Taking a moment to absorb the scene, I can feel the tears prickling in my eyes again. I let that man believe for two years that I didn't love him too. That I wanted to be friends, and nothing more. And here he stands, shrouded in sunlight, waving at me as though his heart isn't broken, as though seeing me doesn't renew his pain.

Unable to keep from him any longer, I storm forward, waving the letter maniacally in my hand.

'I love you, too,' I call out as loudly as I can, despite being out of breath only seconds ago, but Jacob only looks at me perplexed.

'What?' he says with furrowed brows.

I'm close enough to reach out to grab him now. Trying to summon the words again, I begin breathily, 'I love—', before giving up on words entirely, and pressing my lips to his. Without a second thought, he wraps his arms around my waist and lifts me into the back of his truck, pressing his body between my legs. With each second that passes, the intensity grows.

With him smeared in the mud from my run, he pulls away, just as breathless, just as hot.

'I found your letter.' He's close enough that I only need to whisper, and his eyes clear with a look of innocent happiness as the weight of my words finally hits him.

'My letter?'

I nod, holding him by the cheeks. 'I never got it. I must have cleared it away in a rush with all of Granny's things and it's sat in that box ever since.'

His eyes search my face. 'I thought . . . I . . . I waited all day for you. Then I found out you'd already left.' He lets out a breathy laugh. 'I thought I was too late.' Jacob buries his head in my chest, and his warm breath spreads across my body until I curl into the closeness.

'I saw you with Pen that morning,' I explain. 'I went to look for you after I found the other note, and you were there with her. You looked so happy.'

'Other note?' He stands to his full height.

'The note that said "I'm sorry"?'

Jacob shakes his head. 'I went to Pen to break it all off. I knew she liked me and I was worried I'd been leading her on, so I had to set the record straight before I could let myself start anything with you. I had started writing a note, but I couldn't wait. It wasn't fair to not tell Pen in person, so I screwed up the note and I asked her to meet me in the café first thing that morning.'

I shake my head, wishing I could go back and punch sixteen-year-old Ava so hard in the face. 'And all this time . . . ?'

'I thought . . . Well, I thought you just wanted to be friends. I thought if I could keep reminding myself that, I could keep myself away from you. I tried dating Pen again, tried to help you with everything you needed to get away from here . . .'

'Because you thought I wanted to get away from you? From the farm?'

'Because you made it clear that your future is in Milan,' he says softly.

I think about what Mum said this morning. *Love is bigger than any country; it will travel with you. You don't have to leave it behind.*

'Can't I have both?' I ask. Jacob looks at me, confused. 'I love you, Wolfie. I always have. I can't believe I have wasted all these years not telling you, not showing you that I want you – just as much as I want my future in Milan. I've been so wrapped up in my grief, my jealousy . . . I—I've been so stupid. But I want you, if you'll have me.'

Jacob just grins his wide, chipped-tooth grin, and I know his answer already. Entwining my fingers through his hair, I press my lips again to his, and with just that moment of contact, none of it matters any more. All the misunderstandings, all the crossed wires, and the lost time. None of it matters any more as my body presses to his. My soul finds its way home, and my heart is given in its entirety to my best friend.

EPILOGUE

Eight months later

'Alfie, chew with your mouth closed. I've seen cows with better table manners.' Will tosses a napkin at his brother across the dinner table as his mother scolds him in between her giggles.

The whole family are gathered around Grandad's dining table, Sian's lasagne in the middle of us all. Well, it was, until it was ravaged within seconds. Dad had a lot to do with that. The sight of him at the end of the table, tomato sauce staining his lips, laughing with Mum and Dave, fills me with too much joy to complain.

Will and Alfie have done nothing but bicker since they stepped over the threshold, but Grandad joins in on their banter, teasing Will for his wonky drilling of the wheat field, and Will teases him about old Betty in return. Grandad grins like a cheeky teenager; it's like he and Will are mates down the pub with the way they throw their jokes back and forth. It really is a sight to behold. Callum and Lizzie chatter away about whatever the latest *Star Wars* show is and no one bothers to disturb them.

Jacob and I sit together in contented silence. His hand

rests naturally on my thigh as we both watch the scene unfold before us, unable to contain our smiles. 'I'm going to miss this.' I rest my head against his shoulder as I speak, absorbed in the way his thumb runs in circles against my skin.

'Me too,' he murmurs, chipped smile on full display as Grandad flings a lettuce leaf at Alfie, who is too stunned to speak, as the rest of the adults at the table burst out in hysterics. Joy, one of Hope's kittens, weaves around my chair. Both kittens moved into Grandad's house one cold evening without an invite, and despite grumbling about how they smell, or how he has no interest in the animals, Grandad hasn't had the heart to kick them out. They keep each other company. I've often caught the three of them asleep together in his armchair. They make quite the family.

'Right, I think that means it's time for a toast.' Mum stands up with her glass of wine trembling in her hand from her continuing fit of giggles. 'To my baby girl, who spreads her wings next week and starts university in Milan. We are so, so proud of you.' She glances over at Dad, who tries to hide his glassy eyes with a swig from his drink. 'I know Granny would be beside herself with pride. She wouldn't have rested until everyone in the village knew all about you, and I know she will be with you every step of the way, in your heart, and in your sewing machine. I love you.' She doesn't hide her tears as she raises her glass, and I have to catch my own in my napkin.

'To Ava!' The rest of the table repeat after her.

'And of course, I couldn't forget Jacob. Every designer needs her photographer by her side, and my god can this boy take photos. You better look after my little girl out there. I know that as long as she's with you, she's as happy and as safe as can be.' I look up at my boyfriend with pride. A little mud from the orchard still lingers on his neck from earlier in the day, and I blush at the reminder. 'To Jacob.' They all raise their glasses again.

'Can we have pudding now?' Alfie puts an end to the speeches with his request. The clamouring that follows can only be compared to that of hungry pigeons, and Jacob and I take it as our cue to slip out.

Jacob is taking a year to figure out where he wants to be, what he wants to do. He knows his passion lies in photography, but in what capacity, he hasn't quite figured out yet. So, in the coming months, he will come with me to Milan, to explore the city, to put his skills to the test, and to widen his horizons. He's also splitting his time with the farm, not quite ready to let Will be completely in charge just yet.

Like second nature, Jacob and I find our way to the treehouse and clamber up onto the rickety structure. Sat side by side, we both look out at the view beyond the window, as the country stretches for miles and the whole world lies at the end of it.

'It's not too late to run off into the woods, you know.' I nudge Jacob and he wraps his arm around me tightly.

'You know, I think I'm actually starting to enjoy the real world,' he says. 'The woods can wait. We're off to Milan.'

'I love you, Wolfie.'

'I love you, Kitty.'

ACKNOWLEDGEMENTS

It is no understatement that my partner Tom is the reason this book is in existence. In the few months that I was writing this, he carried me as I carried our son. On all of the days I couldn't get out of bed, couldn't wash my own hair, couldn't stomach even a drop of water, he was my body, my voice, my rock. I have no idea how I managed to get any words on a page, but I know that I have Tom to thank for that. He did his best to take away every other burden so the only thing I had to do was grow our boy and type these words. We still have a few months to wait until we get to meet our son, but I can't wait to show him this book, for him to know that his mum never gave up, and that his dad truly is the best of men.

I have to thank my Mum too. Every year I grow, and with every life lesson I am faced with, I learn more about you, and it only makes me love you so much more. You gave us everything growing up, and you still do now. I wouldn't have been a writer without you, and to be held by you, even now at twenty-six years old, is a tonic to even the hardest of life's challenges.

Dad, as always, thank you for being you – aka, me, but with a much wiser head, and a lot less hair. Thank you for always trying to fix every one of my troubles and worries, despite the amount of stress lines I've gifted you over the years. Thank you for always being at the end of the phone to hear me moan, or to bounce around ideas with. I don't know what I'd do without our conversations where it feels as though we are old friends and I always end up wondering if my soul is that of middle-aged bloke, or yours is that of an overly dramatic girl in her twenties. Either way, I know our souls are one and the same.

Thank you to my agents, Florence and Becky – I really wouldn't know where I'd be without you (probably still trying to read through my first contract and make sense of it).

To the whole team at HarperCollins, Electric Monkey, and all of the fantastic freelancers, thank you for working so tirelessly to get this book to this point and beyond. So much more goes into the creation of a book than anyone can truly understand, but your contributions never go unnoticed. Thank you, endlessly: Liz Sellen-Bankes, Arundhati Subhedar, Lindsey Heaven, Beth Mackenzie, Kam Man, Emily Sommerfield, Hannah Penny, Ingrid Gilmore, and Bex Glendining.

And, of course, thank you, reader. For joining my journey, and the journey of these characters, it is all for you. I hope you've found a little slice of home on Hope Farm.

Return to Hope Farm In . . .

The Summer I Saw Him

The Spring I Let You Go

The Winter I Wished For Us

MEGAN CLAWSON

Megan Clawson was born and raised in Boston, Lincolnshire. In 2018, she moved to London to study English with Film at King's College London. The daughter of a Beefeater, Megan lived inside the Tower of London with her dad and little dog, Ethel, for many years. The experience of living inside the real-life palace and fortress still inspires much of her writing. Now she lives back in the peace and quiet of the Lincolnshire countryside with her family, working in a local primary school alongside her writing. *Falling Hard for the Royal Guard* was her debut novel, published in 2023.